D0862072

Books of Merit

cobalt **blue**

mary borsky

. . .

cobalt **blue**

STORIES

thomas allen publishers

toronto

Library and Archives Canada Cataloguing in Publication

Borsky, Mary, 1946–
Cobalt blue : stories / Mary Borsky.

ISBN 978-0-88762-276-2

I. Title.

PS8553.O735C63   2007   C813'.54   C2007-900817-8

"The Ukrainian Shirt," "Wedding Pictures," and "People Like Us" first appeared in *The New Quarterly*, "Ragtime" in *Queen's Quarterly*, "Viewfinder" in *Event*, "Cobalt Blue" in *Malahat Review*.

Editor: Patrick Crean
Cover and text design: Gordon Robertson
Cover image: Karen Beard/Getty Images

Published by Thomas Allen Publishers,
a division of Thomas Allen & Son Limited,
145 Front Street East, Suite 209,
Toronto, Ontario M5A 1E3 Canada

www.thomas-allen.com

  Canada Council for the Arts

The publisher gratefully acknowledges the support of The Ontario Arts Council for its publishing program.

We acknowledge the support of the Canada Council for the Arts, which last year invested $20.0 million in writing and publishing throughout Canada.

We acknowledge the Government of Ontario through the Ontario Media Development Corporation's Ontario Book Initiative.

We acknowledge the financial support of the Government of Canada through the Book Publishing Industry Development Program (BPIDP) for our publishing activities.

11 10 09 08 07   1 2 3 4 5

Printed and bound in Canada

For Soon Jin

"While out there in orbit,
mostly we dreamed of home."

— VLADIMIR LYAKHOV,
COSMONAUT

For kindness, help and humour along the way, I thank Julia Campbell, my writing group, Nancy Baele, Gabriella Goliger, Kim Jernigan, Frances Itani, Sharon Ells, Winkie Fairbairn, Alison Blackburn and Jeff Blackburn. I thank Patrick Crean for his thoughtful editing, and both Patrick Crean and John Metcalf for being fearless champions of the short story. I wish to acknowledge assistance from Canada Council, the Ontario Arts Council, and the City of Ottawa.

"While out there in orbit,
mostly we dreamed of home."

— VLADIMIR LYAKHOV,
COSMONAUT

For kindness, help and humour along the way, I thank Julia Campbell, my writing group, Nancy Baele, Gabriella Goliger, Kim Jernigan, Frances Itani, Sharon Ells, Winkie Fairbairn, Alison Blackburn and Jeff Blackburn. I thank Patrick Crean for his thoughtful editing, and both Patrick Crean and John Metcalf for being fearless champions of the short story. I wish to acknowledge assistance from Canada Council, the Ontario Arts Council, and the City of Ottawa.

contents

cobalt **blue**

the **ukrainian** shirt

The first morning Norman and I were at my mother's, her eavestroughs had to be put up and everyone was mobilizing for it.

My sister-in-law, Bonnie, was flipping pancakes, and my brother, Amel, was eating them, swearing meanwhile on a stack of invisible bibles that he would never vote again now that Trudeau had given the finger to the people of the West.

"The Prime Minister of Canada!" Amel shouted, thumping his hand to his heart. "The man we-the-people put into office! The *Prime Minister*!" He looked around the table to see whether we were following him.

Uncle Walter, who farmed nearby, rubbed his sunburned neck and laughed along in a melancholy way.

Mother was somewhere, likely checking on her potatoes or sweeping glass from the road.

"Have another pancake, Amel my man," Bonnie said in her sparky little way. "It'll make you feel better."

Norman and I were wedged in at one end of the table, both of us wearing green jade wedding bands. We hadn't slept well that first night in my childhood bed.

"I thought Ukrainians would be so different," Norman had complained, turning away from me in bed. "You made them sound so different." He held the bedcovers under his chin and stared up at the cracks in the green ceiling.

"What are you talking about?" I said. I couldn't believe he was saying this. Especially considering how understanding I'd been about his less than perfect manners when we arrived. I hadn't said a word about the way he'd ignored all my relatives and started reading a two-year-old newspaper that was lying on my mother's coffee table.

"You made them sound so extreme," Norman insisted, still holding himself away from me. "So rough and ready. I thought they'd be hanging off the rafters. But they're really quite ordinary."

I decided to switch off the light, which meant I had to get out of bed, thereby banging my ankle on one of the numerous pieces of furniture that were crowded into the room.

Before long, drunks, wandering outside on the street, began yelling in a belligerent but forlorn way, *"Parrr-ty! Parrr-ty!"* I had to get out of bed yet again, clamber through dusty curtains and clattering venetian blinds, to wrestle with the window.

The bed was a double, extremely soft, and Norman and I each hung on to our own side, as if stranded in the middle of the Atlantic on an inadequately inflated life raft.

Toward morning, huge delivery trucks began their incremental and interminable backing into the gigantic 24-hour supermarket that had sprung up across the street from my mother's. At some point Norman and I got dressed, went to the Super-A across the street, where we pushed a cart down the long, chilly aisles until, defeated by an overabundance of choice, we came home with cornflakes and milk.

"Our duly elected Prime Minister!" Amel continued. "He looks out his first-class train window—paid for by *our* taxes!—and gives *us* the finger! Am I the guy who's got it wrong? Am I the guy who's missing something?" He cast a dark and aggrieved look up and down the breakfast table.

"Sure, it's insulting," I said. "Sure it is." I turned to Norman, who usually had plenty to say on topics like this, but this time Norman was silent as the soggy cornflakes before him.

Norman had never met my family all at once and on their own territory before. He was from New Zealand, and had only recently arrived in Canada to study anthropology at UBC and to embark on his life as a world adventurer. His hope was to study different peoples in faraway places, to immerse himself in their ways of life, to learn their languages and study their cultures. Norman's moving into my apartment in Vancouver, where I had a job teaching school, had been mostly his idea, our subsequent marriage mostly mine.

"So, Norman," Uncle Walter said in his polite, self-effacing way. "You're a few miles from home." His faded blue eyes registered mild surprise, as if something about Norman presented a puzzle, but one he expected would resolve itself in due course.

Norman sat up straight, as if called upon in school, and inclined his head quickly toward Uncle Walter. "I beg your pardon?" he said in his Britishey South Seas twang.

"You're a long way from New Zealand," I translated, smiling at Norman to encourage him. I wanted this visit to go well. I wanted my family to like Norman, to think I'd done not too badly. "You're pretty much as far away from New Zealand as you can get," I continued, with yet another smile, "mile-wise, anyway."

"Mile-wise!" Norman echoed, brightening. He turned to me with a show of scholarly interest. "*Mile-wise.* That's fascinating. Tell me, is *mile-wise* a regional expression?" He waited for my reply, holding one finely tapered finger contemplatively in the air.

Everyone stopped chewing and turned to study Norman, taking in his peach-coloured hair and beard, his sharply scissored nose, his hands—now somewhat primly folded on his lap—pink, finely formed, barely bigger than my own. They looked at his green jade wedding band, at his tan plaid shirt, at his khaki shorts.

There was a lengthy silence.

Finally, they returned to their pancakes.

"Now, some guys would throw the eavestroughs up with tin snips and a hammer," Amel announced, washing down his pancakes with coffee. "But I came prepared to do the job right. I brought my acetylene torch, I brought my steel pipes, I brought my crimper, my threader, my cutter. When I do a job, I do it right!"

"Isn't that a fact!" Bonnie said proudly, holding up Amel's well-polished plate for general admiration.

"And don't forget," Mother said, emerging from somewhere with a pail in her hands and what appeared to be a rag around her hair. "Don't forget the pipes for the rain barrels and the cistern." Her face had the pale, caught-off-guard look of a mushroom suddenly held up to the light of day.

Amel remained motionless for a moment. "Let's get one thing straight here," he said slowly, taking time to sift her words for some nugget of offence.

Bonnie refilled Amel's coffee cup, scooped in two spoonfuls of sugar, a dribble of condensed milk, then clinked the spoon in his cup.

Amel pulled his hand across his chin, rasping his whiskers. He shifted his bulky shoulders and raised his eyes to Mother's. "Who's in charge of this job here?" he said. "Me? Or you?"

"I didn't say you'd go and do nothing wrong," Mother said, hunching stubbornly over her pail but looking back at him.

"Irene," Amel demanded, turning to me, "you're the schoolteacher. You choose, Irene. Mom can't make up her mind. Good workmanship or shoddy workmanship?"

"Good sounds good," I said, finding myself springing up to refill my coffee cup at the stove. "Good sounds just fine." I looked over to catch Norman's eye, but Norman was reading the list of ingredients on the back of the pancake syrup. "Don't worry, Mom. They'll do a good job," I added.

"Don't waste my time if you want to settle for something less," Amel rumbled ominously.

"No one's not asking you to do nothing that wastes your precious time," my mother answered, still facing Amel, pale and puffy, from over the top of her bucket.

It was so shadowy in the room, I could barely make out the dirt-covered tubers in the bottom of my mother's pail. The Super-A across the street seemed to block the light from the front and had sent cracks laddering up my mother's kitchen wall.

"Was it always this dark in here?" I asked, looking around the kitchen. "Didn't there used to be more light than this?"

"A cistern!" Amel shouted, laughing to deflect the conversation back to a more friendly footing. "A cistern to hold rainwater! Who else has a cistern these days?" His even white teeth shone in his face. He pushed himself back from the table in a lordly way.

"Look at it, Mom!" he continued. "You got your own self-contained system here! You got your own wood stove!

You got your own cistern! You got your own sauerkraut and canned beets and whatnot! Do you all realize, if we're hit by an atomic bomb, you're going to live a few days longer than the rest of us?!"

Amel's laugh boomed out again. Uncle Walter shook his head and grinned along in an unhappy way.

I poured my cup of coffee into the sink and began to stack the dirty plates while Amel, Uncle Walter, Mother and Bonnie tramped noisily outside to survey the eavestrough project. Already, Norman had pulled a paperback from his back pocket and was reading, his bare legs crossed, his book angled toward the net-curtained window.

I looked at him. The book was called *Head-hunters of Central Borneo*.

I looked outside the kitchen windows. The breeze through the screen had a slightly metallic smell. Amel, Bonnie, Uncle Walter and Mother were standing in a row facing the kitchen window and looking up. I saw Uncle Walter point, heard him say something, heard everyone laugh.

I turned to Norman, hugging my elbows, rocking lightly on my feet. "Norman," I asked, as brightly as I could, "are you going to go out and give them a hand?"

Norman stopped reading and looked up with a start.

"Me?" he said. *"Now?"*

•   •   •

Through my mother's orange net kitchen curtains, I was aware of men's voices, of pipes passing through the air, of the positioning of a plank horizontally outside the kitchen window.

I washed the dishes quickly, leaving them to air-dry. My mother, who did not trust any avoidance of work, even unnecessary work, had never air-dried a dish in her life, or even soaked a pot to make the scrubbing of it easier. Nothing was done right unless it was done the hard way.

I wiped off the stove, taking more time with it than I ordinarily would, pushed a broom across the linoleum, examined the cracks in the front room ceiling. Anything to avoid looking out the kitchen window.

When at last I could take the suspense no longer, I pushed the kitchen curtains aside and saw Amel's yellow work boots on the right end of the plank, Uncle Walter's darker shoes close beside. After a tense lapse, I spotted Norman's brand new white runners on the opposite end of the plank.

Something like a stone lifted off my chest, releasing me, releasing the sun, in fact, for at that moment a shaft of sunlight pierced the room, making the kitchen more roomy and cheerful, making the world a more hopeful and habitable place after all.

Husband, I found myself thinking as I polished the knobs and faucet of the stainless steel sink to a shine. *Husband.* I liked the word, which suggested to me a certain safely harnessed male energy, something dark, polished, valuable: a mahogany dining table, for example, or a shiny-rumped Clydesdale. *Wife*, on the other hand, I reflected, I did not like nearly so well, sounding as it did so, well . . . *wifey*.

As I folded the dishrag and draped it over the faucet, I thought that from the corner of my eye I caught a glimpse of the Ukrainian shirt I'd made for Norman. But when I pushed the curtains aside and looked more closely, I saw Norman was wearing the same ordinary tan plaid shirt he'd worn at breakfast. It made sense that Norman hadn't run in to change his shirt in the middle of putting up the eavestroughs. Besides, I didn't know if Norman had even brought the shirt I'd made for him.

Then, moments later, at the edge of my field of vision, I once more saw the flash of unbleached linen, blue and tan embroidered flowers—Norman's Ukrainian shirt. So he *was* wearing it, I thought.

But when I peered out a second time, I found that, for the second time, I was mistaken.

•   •   •

I'd made Norman the Ukrainian shirt for his birthday. Sewing had never been a strength of mine, but I had taken three years of high school home ec, and in my final year made the two-piece, fully lined, brown wool suit that I wore the first day of teachers' training. Since that time, though,

I hadn't done much sewing, apart from very infrequently machine-stitching a cushion. Still, I passed a fabrics store every day on my way home from school, and the notion of making a shirt for Norman tugged at me.

After studying the patterns for men's shirts, the one that most appealed to me was a Cossack-styled shirt, a basic straight-cut man's shirt with a front slit at the neck and a mandarin collar. I chose a good grade of unbleached linen to cut it from, and machine-embroidered strips of tan and blue flowers to sew around the neckline and the cuffs.

I worked on the shirt in the evenings while Norman was at the library, no light in the room except for the small yellow pool cast by the light of the sewing machine itself, no sound but the crinkle of tissue paper and the quick metallic clatter of the machine. I joined small dots to small dots, big dots to big dots, and sewed French seams throughout, happy in my own little world of cutting, pinning, ripping and sewing.

"You made this?" Norman asked when I presented the shirt to him at his birthday dinner. "Yourself?"

He examined the shirt under the reading lamp, then pulled it on when I urged him to. He looked down at it, smiling uncertainly, stretching his arms to see the strip of embroidery around the cuffs.

"My father was wearing a shirt like that in his immigration photo," I said. "Only his would have been hand-done. Even the linen. Can you imagine the work?"

Candlelight shone steadily from the table and again, but more erratically, from the ceiling, which I'd covered with aluminum foil to offset the gloom of the west coast climate. Until I'd met Norman, I'd been plotting my escape back to the Prairies, but now the rain, the damp, the porridge skies didn't seem to have anything much to do with me. Those things seemed like something happening outside the window. They seemed like weather.

"I'll have to save this for a special occasion," Norman said carefully. He looked down at the shirt again. He was still holding his arms straight out.

I cut myself another sliver from the birthday cake, which I'd also made from scratch, carrot with cream cheese icing.

"It's a casual style," I explained happily. "It's a peasant shirt. It's the kind of shirt you can wear anywhere."

•   •   •

Chuloveek, I remembered, was the Ukrainian word for husband. It had, to my ear, a more forceful, less tameable sound than the more smoothly rounded *husband*. This was the kind of thing Norman would find interesting, and I made a mental note to mention this to him later.

Husband, chuloveek, I said to myself, *chuloveek, husband.* I was balancing the words like balls of bread dough in my hands when Mother and Bonnie came back into the kitchen, each of them carrying a pail of pin cherries. Mother looked around, surveying the damage I'd done to her kitchen, then brushed past me to pull her colander from the cupboard.

"Well, Norman looks about as happy as a drowned cat!" Bonnie announced, pretending to laugh but her eyes sparking darkly.

Mother and Bonnie turned together and thundered their pin cherries into the sink, their feet side by side, Bonnie's ample blue-jeaned hips lined up beside my mother's more scrawny ones, their shoulders and heads tilted at the exact same working angle over the berries. I'd always told myself that the reason I couldn't work with Mother was that she was impossible to work with, that she had no clear system of doing things, that she expected you to read her mind. But Bonnie, who was born in Lebanon, knew instinctively how to work with her.

I made my way out through the oven-hot porch, which smelled faintly of pesticides.

Outside, the blinding midday sun made something behind my eyes clench into a fist. I walked to the side of the house, shielded my eyes with both hands against the brilliant sky, and looked up at the men at work on the plank.

Amel and Uncle Walter still stood on one end, talking in their easy working way as they raised the eavestrough to the edge of the roof. At the other end, Norman, bare-legged, stood alone, his figure slight, his shoulders sagging. He was holding the dangling end of the eavestrough in his hands.

Whatever it was that Norman should be doing, it was clear he wasn't doing it. Shouldn't he be, for instance, holding the eavestrough *up*? It didn't seem to serve any purpose to hold it while it was dangling down like that. Why didn't Amel or Uncle Walter tell him what to do? Why didn't Norman, for that matter, *ask*?

I felt a little dizzy. My skin felt tight and hot. Norman looked as dejected as a prisoner of war, but I found it impossible to pity him, the way he submitted to the weight of the pipe and did not in any way exert himself against it.

I walked quickly around the house to the grove of pin cherries, but I stood there only a moment before a man I'd noticed hanging around the Dumpster outside the Super-A ambled amicably in my direction. By his sedate low-slung belly, I recognized him as one of the drunks who'd kept us awake the night before. The man started to touch the peak of his baseball cap, as if he was about to say something, but I was already turning to go back inside the house.

In the darkened front room where Norman and I left our suitcases, I spilled out my hairbrush, shampoo, toothpaste, then suddenly—sensing someone in the shadows behind me—spun around, my heart slamming hard in my chest.

It was Norman. Norman was sitting in an armchair in the shadows, a book almost to his face. He couldn't have been in the house longer than a minute or two.

"This is fascinating," he said, raising an eyebrow. "The system of marriage among the Australian Aborigines is considerably more complicated than ours." He looked at me as if inviting a response. "Everything is based upon what clan or section or subsection you belong to, and you can or cannot marry into other clans or sections or subsections according to a complicated set of rules, including agreements that may have been made before you were born. The system is so complicated, even a mathematician can have trouble with it."

I stared at Norman for a moment. "Did we bring Aspirin?" I asked, dumping my underwear onto the floor.

In my chest and arms I still felt the shock of sensing a dark figure in the shadows behind me. Sometimes drunks came into my mother's house. Mother had found one sitting in the porch, another time she'd found one asleep on the couch. She called the RCMP, who drove down to pick them up and to sympathize with her. "You shouldn't have to put up with that," the RCMP officer said, and Mother liked to tell about it, about what had happened, the kindness of the young RCMP officer and what exactly he'd said to her.

In the kitchen, Bonnie, who was standing at the stove in front of a steaming pot of pin cherries, had a snappy smile for me. "I see Norman's reading again," she said.

"He has a paper due," I said, though I wasn't aware of any paper. I passed between Bonnie and my mother, who was pouring boiling water into glass jars on the table.

"Does he always read in the dark like that?" Mother asked,

the large aluminum kettle still in her hands. She looked through the cloud of steam toward the darkened doorway to the front room. "Tell him he can turn on the light if he wants to."

•   •   •

The Super-A across the street had part of a brightly lit aisle devoted to headache remedies. I selected the most potent-looking, and took two tablets even before I passed through the cash.

I bypassed the in-house coffee counter and walked down the block to a real coffee shop, where I seated myself at a small table along the wall.

I watched the waitress fill my cup from a prepared pot and admired the geometric order of the tables and chairs, each place set with a paper placemat, a serviette holder and ketchup at the side. Behind the counter, a coffee machine shone and hummed. Lemon meringue pies, butter tarts and jewel-coloured bowls of Jell-O were brilliantly illuminated inside a glass case.

Three men at a window table were talking about fencing, the cost of different wires, the advantage of page-lock versus hinge-lock.

"You drill your posts two feet deep, run hinge-lock along the top, a strand of electric wire, and you got yourself a fence," one of the men said.

"It's going to run you anywheres from four dollars a foot up," another added.

I felt something inside my brain unfold and take its proper shape. What a relief not to be hearing about marriage systems of the Australian Aborigines, kinship lines of the Kwakiutl or taboos of the Trobriand Islanders.

Give me real things any day, I thought.

But then I slipped back to an unhappy, mismatched feeling inside my head. It felt like I was trying to sew the sleeve of a shirt in backwards and hadn't admitted the mistake to myself yet. I kept searching about for some piece of solid truth in all this.

Norman hadn't helped Amel and Uncle Walter, I told myself, but I wasn't exactly up to my eyeballs in jams and jellies along with Bonnie, was I?

Besides, the Trobriand Islanders were likely real enough, I supposed, once you got to the Trobriand Islands.

I could feel my banished headache open one bleary eye, like an improperly anaesthetized patient. When the waitress came by, I let her refill my coffee cup.

There was, I finally decided, only one fact in this entire array of events that held its shape no matter which way I looked at it.

This was that fact: *It would not have killed Norman to help with the eavestroughs.*

•   •   •

As I approached my mother's house again, I saw the blue flame of Amel's welder, saw my mother pouring water from her aluminum kettle into the cup of a man who was standing on the other side of the fence. When I got closer, I saw it was the nighttime drunk who'd tried to talk to me earlier.

"I thought you didn't want them to come around," I said to my mother. "You shouldn't encourage them."

"They get tea bags from the Dumpster. Why not give them hot water?" she said.

"Get a shot of this top corner, Bonnie," Amel called out to his wife, who was snapping pictures. "Look at this! Isn't this a beauty? Pass me the camera! I got to get a picture of the bonnet!

"Feel it," Amel invited Mother. "It's solid as a rock! You could do chin-ups on these eavestroughs!" He was, again, standing on the plank.

I saw that he'd made a complicated system, anchoring the eavestroughs to steel posts on each corner of the house. The eavestroughs themselves were galvanized tin, but reinforced underneath with long thin steel pipes, while wider steel pipes went down into the rain barrels.

"These eavestroughs are going to be here after the rest of us are dust!" Amel yelled happily.

"Why did you put something over the top like that?" Mother asked, squinting up at the eavestroughs. She was still holding the aluminum kettle. "How's the rain supposed to get in?"

"The rain can still get in," Amel said.

"I want it the way it used to be," Mother said, pushing against the steel drainpipe. "And why are those ugly posts at the corners? They're not going to stay there, are they? I thought they were just here to get the other part up!"

"What's the matter?" Amel said, his face tumbling down into a pudding. He held his hands toward her, palms upward. "You like cleaning eavestroughs? I made it so you will never need to clean an eavestrough again!"

Mother pushed against the drainpipe a second time, looked up to see the entire structure.

"I did something *good* for you," Amel said, looking down at her from the plank.

Uncle Walter, who was standing beside me now, rubbed his cheek mournfully.

Mother put the kettle on the ground, pulled the rag from her head.

I could see last night's reveller sitting on the curb across the street, drinking his tea from a Styrofoam cup and apparently considering the newly installed eavestrough system. Norman was out now too, nodding to himself as he looked at the completed project. He put his arm around me and smiled down in a complicit way.

"Look!" Amel said, his voice hearty again. "It's one self-referential system! It's a masterpiece!"

"How can I get it apart?" Mother asked, still pushing at the pipe that went into the rain barrel.

"You can't! That's the beauty of it! It's cast in steel now!"

"What if a stick gets in?" Mother was crying now, her grey hair streaming down around her face. "How am I supposed to get a stick out? I didn't ask you to do it this way!"

"A stick's not going to get in," Amel explained. "That's the whole thing about the bonnet. Rainwater gets in, but sticks and leaves and dead birds stay out." He jumped to the ground with surprising lightness for a man his size. "I guarantee it, Mom," he said, his arm around her shoulder.

She wouldn't answer.

"Anyway, it was Irene's idea," he said at last, half winking at me.

"Mine?"

"Sure." Amel grinned. "You said do a good job. Look," he said, turning to Mother, "I'll paint them green to match your trim."

"I don't want them green," Mother answered.

"A nice bright yellow," Amel countered. "Irene, you're the schoolteacher. What do you think of a nice bright yellow?"

"I don't want them yellow," Mother said. "I want them how they are."

"See?" Amel said with a show of joviality. "She wants them how they are."

•　　•　　•

"You planning on moving back to Australia?" Uncle Walter asked Norman. His manner was as quiet and as courteous as ever, but I thought I detected a thin shadow of judgment in his blue eyes.

We were in the kitchen eating supper, which had turned out to be a bucket of Kentucky Fried Chicken from the outlet on the highway.

"We haven't discussed going to Australia, have we, Norman?" I said. "Anyway, Norman's not from Australia. He's from New Zealand."

Amel leaned back on his chair, a pleasant expression on his face. "Norman comes from Australia," Amel said. He was speaking directly to me. Amel had a bottle of beer in his hand, several under his belt, was pleased with the eavestroughs and was settling into the mood for an argument.

"Norman doesn't come from Australia," I said.

"Norman comes from Australia," Amel insisted.

"Norman doesn't come from Australia. Norman comes from New Zealand."

"Australia. Norman comes from Australia."

"New Zealand!" I said, laughing now. "I must know where my own husband comes from!" I shook my head. I couldn't tell if he was joking.

"But you said Norman came from Australia," Amel said, knitting his brow as if deeply perplexed.

"No, I didn't. I said Norman comes from New Zealand!"

Laughing again, I turned to Norman, but Norman wasn't laughing.

Headlights from a truck outside flashed across the kitchen.

"New Zealand, Australia," Amel said magnanimously. "Why didn't you say so? New Zealand, Australia, big difference."

"Maybe he likes it better in Austrillia," my mother said darkly.

I unscrewed the top of another beer, reached over to refill Norman's glass.

"I should love to return to New Zealand," Norman said, his features tightening but his pupils large and dark with hope. "But there are also a number of other countries I intend to experience first-hand."

It was silent in the room, and I realized I was afraid Norman would go on to talk about his dreams of seeing the world, of living with different peoples, learning their ways and going on to write about his observations and experiences. I didn't think my family would think less of him for those dreams, no less than they did now. They would likely see such notions as odd and far-fetched, but not exactly surprising in a man who was unwilling to pitch in to put up an eavestrough.

It was for my own sake that I didn't want to hear Norman talk about those dreams right now. His dreams suddenly seemed to be insubstantial, cobwebby things. They seemed better talked about far away, by candlelight, under an aluminum foil ceiling. I didn't think I could bear to examine Norman's dreams just then, not by the unforgiving fluorescent light of my mother's kitchen.

I could feel Norman looking at me. I placed the ketchup, vinegar, evaporated milk, the salt and pepper in a careful line, largest to smallest, in the middle of the table.

"Listen!" Amel said softly. He held up his hand. "Listen. Do you hear that?"

We sat quietly.

Outside, there was the soft blast of rain on the roof, then the first slow trickle of rainwater running down into the cistern.

•   •   •

Norman wore the Ukrainian shirt a few times, once to an anthropology department party where another graduate student, when she learned I was teaching school, said in a show-offy voice, "How very *brave* of you!"

The shirt was really too big for Norman, too long in the arms and so baggy in the neck it made his throat look thin. But with the embroidered strips already sewn on, it would have been a lot of work to take it in.

Norman took to sleeping late in the mornings. One day, as I was leaving for school and Norman was still snoring,

I walked over to his dresser, pulled his Ukrainian shirt out of the drawer and tried to tear it into pieces.

But with the high-quality fabric I'd used, and the French seams I'd sewn throughout, the shirt wouldn't give anywhere. Finally, in my fury, I stood on a sleeve, yanked and heard the fabric rip.

Shocked by the sound, I immediately looked over at Norman, then down at the shirt. Norman only frowned and kept sleeping, but fabric of the shirt had given along one of the side seams, though it still hung together with the horizontal threads. I remembered that the vertical and horizontal threads were called woof and warp, but I could no longer remember which was which.

I stared at the shirt, then refolded it and put it back into Norman's drawer.

Later that day, Norman noticed the tear and seemed to guess how it had happened, even before I had a chance to blame the washing machine. Holding the shirt in one hand, he leaned toward me, slightly embarrassed, and kissed me.

I was embarrassed too, being caught out in this way. I said I might be able to mend the shirt. The tear was not that visible, and the fit might even be improved by being taken in a little. Norman agreed that the shirt looked mendable and I put it into the African basket where I stored the undone mending.

I never did get around to repairing the shirt, though, and one of the times I left, while I was waiting for the taxi, I dumped the unappreciated Ukrainian shirt with its tan and blue flowers into a black garbage bag.

The gift that had not been a true gift after all.

I had thought to take the African basket for myself, but there was a pain in the exact centre of my chest, the taxi was honking, and it was all I could manage to pull on my raincoat, pick up the suitcase I'd packed, then step out into the thick, wet Vancouver fog.

wedding **pictures**

Kerry gave Randall his gift at supper, a coffee mug that had a picture of a green man with his hair combed straight back. The green man's name was *Mr. Fussy*.

They'd just finished a dinner Kerry had prepared from scratch, linguine with clam sauce (a recipe recommended by the other nurses in the cardiac unit), also Caesar salad with homemade dressing—no small feat in Randall's small and sparsely equipped kitchen.

She'd fed her four-year-old daughter, Mackenzie, earlier and settled her in front of Randall's television with her old baby blanket and a bag of Gummi Bears. Tomorrow would be taken up with preparing for Randall's photo exhibition at the local gallery and framing store, then, by mid-afternoon, she and Mackenzie would have to set out on their drive back to Calgary. She wouldn't see Randall for at least two weeks, at which point it would be his turn to do the driving.

What she wanted was to have tonight to themselves.

"Fussy," Randall said, his pie-shaped face genial but slightly baffled. He blew out the candles in the centre of the table, smiled a trifle uncertainly, adjusted his glasses. Light from the front room caught on the crate of bubble-wrapped photographs in the doorway, glinted off the edge of his metal frames. "That's the supposition here, am I correct? That I'm fussy?"

"But cute," Kerry laughed, leaning over to kiss him. "You're cute too."

"What's going on in here?" a small, pale-blanketed figure demanded, gliding into the room. She opened the refrigerator, then turned to stare at them from its lit doorway.

Kerry folded her hands on her lap. "Nothing, sweetie," she said with a huge bright smile.

"Nothing, officer, I swear," Randall added.

"Randall!" Kerry laughed, jostling against his arm. She turned to Mackenzie. "Randall's teasing, sweetheart, that's all."

"How come you laugh whenever Randall says something?" Mackenzie accused, her small face a dark cloud of judgment within the illuminated halo of her wild blonde hair. "You don't laugh at home."

"I don't?" Kerry considered this, then set it carefully aside, like a handful of bills from the mailbox. "Is that true? I don't laugh at home?" She reached forward to tidy Mackenzie's hair, but Mackenzie pulled back.

"No."

Randall bobbed a fish-shaped oven mitt, a gift from a previous visit, over the lip of the table and spoke for it from the edge of his mouth.

"No laughing at all?" the fish inquired, mushing its face together in a goofy way.

"No."

"Not even an inchy-pinchy smile?" the fish teased, turning its head to look at her with one knobbly eye.

Mackenzie took a can of pop from the fridge, handed it to her mother, who snapped it open and gave it back to her.

"No," Mackenzie said, and with her ragged baby blanket cloaking her shoulders, her can of pop in front of her, her back erect, she returned to the living room.

• • •

He and Kerry were good together, Randall thought as he made his way down the stairs to his basement darkroom. From the way she butted her head into his shoulder to laugh, to the way she folded herself so easily into him, everything between them was easy.

The only glitch being, of course, Mackenzie. Half the time Kerry seemed to walk on eggshells around the girl, while the rest of the time she acted like another kid right along with her.

He switched on a lamp and examined the photograph he'd framed earlier. Then he slipped it into a crate of photos and carried it up the narrow stairs with him.

Kerry and Mackenzie. Even putting those names side by side—*Kerry and Mackenzie*—he could feel Kerry sliding away from him, the fragment of a dream, a silk scarf on a windy day. They didn't even talk properly half the time, but used their own sign language, as if the girl were incapable of normal speech. Arms out meant one thing, fingers on the lips something else. A scuffle of the feet, fingers walking up an arm, meant other things. He would have nothing to do with it. No wonder the child was sulky and uncommunicative.

Children need to be spoken to properly, he told himself. They need to know someone's in charge. They need to be told to comb their hair. They need to be told they are too old for a baby blanket. People weren't meant to bump around together like dumb animals in the dark.

When he tried to explain this to Kerry, though—they were in the car, returning from a movie—she looked abruptly out the window at the lanes of oncoming traffic, swift-moving rivers of light and steel.

"You don't understand," she said, her voice barely audible, her half-averted face a pale coin in the flickering darkness of the car. "It's been her and me, together so long, through thick and thin, just the two of us." She looked over her shoulder at him, but offered nothing more.

For some reason, Randall found himself picturing a pink

cloud of cotton candy above a mountain, the sort of thing that decorates the walls of Chinese restaurants.

Then he got it. The cloud and the mountain.

Under the softness, the sweetness, at least where Mackenzie was concerned, Kerry was immovable.

• • •

Kerry first met Randall at her own wedding. She was the bride, an elaborate meringue of satin, lace and pearls, and Randall, sweating and criss-crossed with cameras, was the photographer.

Kerry was marrying Gordon, who was tall, shaggy, Irish wolfhound handsome, with eyes, hair and beard the colour of tarnished pennies. *I am marrying him,* Kerry kept saying to herself, conjugating the marriage into existence. *I am marrying him; he is marrying me; we are getting married.* At one point during the reception, though, she turned to take his hand and he was gone.

It's just nerves, she told herself, scanning the room while she smiled and pretended to everyone—including herself—that everything was all right. She'd known Gordon since high school, and had been secretly in love with him even back then. She knew him, and she was sure (almost completely sure) that this was just wedding day jitters.

Two hours later, Gordon was back. He'd gone out for a cigarette with one of the wedding guests (the red-haired woman in the green suit), and they'd happened upon the tail end of a volleyball tournament, he explained, regaling the entire table with his antics. He'd felt called upon to show the losing team a certain secret counter-manoeuvre, the only thing that could have saved them, but *still* they lost!

Kerry laughed along with the others, not simply a good sport, though she knew a bit about that. In this case, though, she was operating off what she believed was a deeper sense of him. Gordon was a large-scale man, a freewheeling man, a man she loved and trusted, but he was not a man who could be expected to follow all the finer points of social convention.

I'm in for a hard ride, Kerry told herself as they sat laughing together at the banquet table. By *hard*, she meant also *thrilling*. Her marriage to Gordon would be a grand union, she told herself, as challenging, bracing and large-scale as Gordon himself.

Later, when Kerry tried to recall Randall at the wedding, she remembered a shadowy figure, a man with smudged glasses and bedecked with cameras, a man dressed in dark, half-rumpled clothes who hovered around the edges of things.

"Please look at the wineglass and smile," Randall requested, exacting and impersonal as a shoe salesman. He was known for a particular style of wedding photo he did. He could show a bride dancing on a cloud, or a bridegroom looking broodingly into his goblet and seeing the face of his beloved reflected in the glass. Why, Kerry told herself later,

Randall could probably have come up with a bridegroom who accompanied his bride the entire way through their wedding reception!

It was peak season for weddings, Randall told Kerry when she booked him. He had another wedding scheduled that same day, two more the following day. Later, thinking back, Kerry remembered the whirring and clicking of the camera, Randall's round sweaty face, his matter-of-fact voice. "Please, gaze up at the clouds. Don't look. Don't stare. *Gaze.*"

•   •   •

"That *stupid* stream and that *stupid* rainbow," Kerry accused Randall four years later. It was one in the morning and she was calling on her cellphone from a snowy parking lot in Calgary. "Oh. What's the time? Sorry. Did I wake you?"

She'd been standing before the cash register of an all-night drugstore, buying Tempera for Mackenzie, who had an ear infection. She'd been balancing Mackenzie on her hip and fishing for coins trapped between the receipts in her wallet when she'd seen a tattered advertisement on the wall at the cashier's elbow.

Mirror Images, Your Wedding Photo Specialist, the advertisement read. Below were photographs from her and Gordon's wedding.

Her fingers skittered like mice in her wallet and her cheekbones burned. There they were, she and Gordon, hand in hand on a bridge, staring into the mist on the shore beyond. (So *this* is what that mist contained!) Next, they were dancing on a pastel-coloured rainbow. Then there she was again, with her fuller sweeter younger face, smiling prettily down at a tiny tuxedoed Gordon, whom she held on the palm of her hand.

Gordon was long gone from the marriage at this point, though Kerry had been the one to leave, twice. She left him on their wedding night when he told her that he had not wanted to go through with the wedding after all, but that his father convinced him it was too late to change his mind. She left him again, and for good this time, just before Mackenzie was born, when Gordon got a middle-of-the-night phone call from a woman he worked with, and Kerry, lying in bed with her palms pressed to her belly, heard him talking in the bathroom, where he'd barricaded himself with the phone. "No. *No*," she heard him saying in his old passionate way. "*You're* the one. *You're* the one."

"Where did you ever come up with a bridge like that?" Kerry demanded, wiping her nose with a Kleenex. "A white-latticed footbridge! Rainbows! I mean, *rainbows*? Give me a break!"

Randall sent a potted plant over the next day, a blue azalea, and a few weeks later, when he was in Calgary, took Kerry to supper.

He could have sworn he'd taken all the old advertising down, he apologized. He wasn't even photographing weddings anymore. He was photographing pure optical illusions now—floating balls, wood blocks with impossible shadows, triangles that tricked your eye into believing two mutually impossible things at the same time.

"Like your brides and grooms!" Kerry pointed out, laughing a trifle hysterically. "I mean, look at Gordon and me!"

Kerry couldn't help talking too much about Gordon, but it didn't seem to matter. Randall wanted to talk about Oonah, who'd left him for no reason he could decipher. He'd been working toward a deadline, went out at midnight to express-mail his proofs, and when he came back, Oonah was gone.

"Oonah?" said Kerry, not sure she'd heard the name before.

"It's an old Irish name. *Oonah.* Beautiful, isn't it? And it suits her to a T." Then he repeated the name again, slowly, enunciating carefully, in case she hadn't caught it properly the first few times. *"Oooo-nah."*

Randall began to call Kerry in the evenings to chat, and when he was in Calgary took her out to dinner and a movie. He told her how much he liked seeing her. He told her what a difference she made in his life. He photographed her, in a fifties-style diner, standing at a bus stop, and on the Bow River Bridge.

Then she wouldn't hear from him, or see him, for weeks.

She checked the numbers on her call display. She checked her telephone jacks to make sure they were plugged in properly. She dreamed he gave her his camera and that she forgot it on the bus. Then she couldn't remember the number of the bus, find the bus station in the phone book or, for that matter, find a telephone. She woke in a panic.

"It's time to take the bull by the horns," another nurse in the cardiac unit advised.

"Or by some other part of his anatomy," another added. The single and divorced nurses would joke around in this way. Those who were married did not seem to have to talk so boisterously or laugh quite so uproariously.

"You drop in on him one evening. You just happen to be in Edmonton. Why not?"

They helped Kerry with her hair and makeup.

In the time since Kerry married, left Gordon, gave birth to Mackenzie, got through nurse's training and shepherded Mackenzie through ear infections and potty training, eyeshadow had gone from blue to bronze and, in some cases, back to blue again. Lipstick from pink to chocolate to brick. Soft was out! Glitter was in! Even those with an eye for it said it was practically a part-time job, just keeping up.

One of the cardiac care nurses lent her a slinky top and fire-engine red pumps. Someone in her carpool lent her a fake leopard-skin fur coat. Kerry, starting to catch on, bought tight jeans and an underwire bra.

"Okay. I knock. He answers. What do I say?"

"You don't need to say anything. Just look at him and smile."

"I'll bake some bread and take that over," Kerry said.

"*No* bread! *No* cake! *No* cookies! You want to look *desirable*, not *useful*!"

So maybe *this* is what she'd been doing wrong. She'd been baking too much bread! "Desirable. Not useful," Kerry drilled herself, sweating lightly now.

Kerry left Mackenzie with a neighbour, drove three and a half hours to Edmonton, then stopped at a gas station near Randall's to touch up her makeup, slip on her flattering new jeans, exchange her runners for red heels. When she went into the office to return the key, she glanced into the front window and saw the reflection of a woman who was a stranger to her. She saw a woman full of life, colour, movement, a woman with dark lips, bright heels and a fur coat. A bold, carefree, vibrant woman, the sort of woman who didn't think twice about dropping in on her boyfriend if she felt like it.

She tossed her hair over her upturned fur collar, admiring the effect in her rear-view mirror, then pulled out of the gas station with a flourish. (So this is what other women had been doing while she'd been scraping Cheerios off the floor and watching *Mr. Dressup*!)

But Randall's house, when she pulled up, was dark, his car gone. She sat outside, nibbling at her nail polish, breathing mist onto her windows.

It was unthinkable to turn back now. Her new incarnation was too fresh, too fragile, to wrap in tissue paper and tuck into a drawer for another occasion. The wings might crumple. The paint might smear. The entire creation could simply glom up together like Halloween candy left in the back of a cupboard. Besides, things between Randall and her had reached an impasse. They were a rocket ship that had to burst through the earth's atmosphere or break apart trying. They were the bunny that had to pop out of the magician's hat or plain suffocate to death.

Had she misread? Was Randall gay? Was he involved with someone else? She didn't think so.

They were a Christmas cactus that had to bloom or get tossed in the trash.

She locked the car and tried Randall's front door, which was, of course, locked. She tried slipping a credit card into the lock, a trick Randall himself taught her, worrying aloud, as he had, about burglaries.

The door fell open.

Kerry heard her heels on the floor, felt about on the wall for the light switch, snapped it on. She looked about.

There were several straight-back wooden chairs flush against the wall, an austere couch, an end table with a lamp and a black dial telephone. A neat-as-a-pin decor apparently inspired by *The Grapes of Wrath*. She couldn't help glancing out the window, where she half expected to see a rusty old truck rattling past in a Depression-era dust storm.

She placed the bottle of champagne she'd brought beside the phone (impossible to arrive at the door empty-handed), then settled herself on the hard bachelor couch, pulling her coat around herself for warmth while she considered what, if anything, to do next.

Her heart was thumping about in her rib cage and her cheeks felt hot. She was as jumpy as if she had to sing or dance at a school recital, but she was elated too.

Look! She bounced up to examine a photograph of herself that Randall had framed and put on his mantelpiece. The photograph was a bit blurred about the edges, catching her as she'd turned to him, her hair untidy, her eyes slightly hooded. Why hadn't he framed the good one where she was smiling and looked a tiny bit like Cate Blanchett?

Still. From what she could make out, she was in the place of honour, the middle, between two other photographs, a staircase of dominoes and a pyramid of yellow rubber duckies. She did a little triumphal stamp, almost twisting her ankle in the unaccustomed heels, then collapsed back again onto the horsehair couch.

A cup of tea would be nice, she decided. But the only tea to be found in Randall's kitchen was a herbal concoction called *Think O2*. The fridge contained chocolate milk and a nearly empty box of diet cookies. She'd just have to open the champagne then, wouldn't she? (How much simpler life was when a girl had a new hairdo and a pair of red heels!)

The champagne was both tart and sweet, and went down as easily as apple juice.

Kerry poured herself a second glass.

She nibbled at Randall's diet cookies, refreshed her glass, took both the wineglass and the remainder of the bottle with her when she went upstairs to pee.

What she would really like, after her long drive, was a nice hot bubble bath. But she couldn't just help herself to a bath in someone else's house.

Or could she? Randall was not, after all, *someone else.* Randall was the man she was crazy about. And she was the bright bold apparition she'd seen reflected in the gas station window. She was alive, she was free, she belonged to herself.

If Randall came home early?

Randall was a big boy. She was sure he could cope.

Should she leave a note? No, the red heels at the base of the stairs (one of them suggestively on its side), the fur coat tossed alluringly over the banister, would be enough.

She found a candle—citronella, but it would have to do. She ran a bath, made bubbles from Randall's no-name shampoo, hung her slinky top and expensive jeans on the door hook. She climbed into the warm bubbles, slipped her shoulders down into the water. It was years since she'd had a bubble bath on her own, almost as long since she'd been able to lean back and do absolutely nothing.

She felt as though she'd already embarked upon a new life. A new life that involved, among other things, lounging in candlelit bubble baths while she waited for the man of her life to come home. She sipped the champagne and observed how each wiggle of her newly painted toes popped more and more of the hard little shells that seemed to have formed around each of the cells in her body.

She was startled by a sudden sound. *Whump.*

"Hul-lo?" It was Randall's voice from downstairs.

There was a silence, a sense of frosty air. Kerry sat up, placed her wineglass on the edge of the sink and quickly assessed her situation. She reached for Randall's skimpy, threadbare towel.

Yikes! she thought, ducking back down into bathwater. What if he thought she was Oonah! What a joke on herself it would be if the leopard-patterned coat and the fire-engine red heels brought that paragon, Oonah, to mind!

Downstairs, Randall cleared his throat. "Someone there?"

"Hi Randall!" Kerry called, her voice as cheerful and Teflon-coated as a games show hostess. "I'm just having a bath, Randall. Down in a sec!" She made an elucidating splash with the bathwater. Gone was the sultry voice she'd practised in the car. Gone was the mystique she convinced herself she'd contrived. Gone was every shred of confidence she'd ever had in this entire enterprise. She was just Kerry. A loyal friend, a good listener, nice, nice, nice. What a mistake to pretend to be somebody different!

"Holy Toledo, Kerry!" Randall hollered when he flicked on the light in the hallway. He clutched his chest and gasped aloud dramatically. "I'm going to wind up in your cardiac ward, Kerry! Truthfully speaking, that's how I envisage myself!"

"Well, excuse me!" Kerry snapped, lifting her leg from the now-chilly bathwater and shoving the door shut with her foot. She heaved herself from the depleted bubbles, knocking the citronella candle into the bath, where it extinguished itself with a quick, angry hiss. "It's not like I'm having a barrel of laughs either!"

What a fuddy-duddy he'd turned out to be! She'd seen the signs before, but had foolishly ignored them! She had goosebumps and her hands and her feet were hopelessly pruned. She also had a crick in her neck, not to mention a low-grade headache, no doubt from the smell of the photography chemicals Randall stored under the sink.

"Haven't you heard of being *spontaneous*, Randall?" she called through the door. "This is called *Being Spontaneous*!" She stuffed her lacy underwear into her purse, zipped it tight, then proceeded to wedge herself into her one-size-too-small blue jeans. Never again, she told herself. Never again would she pay eighty dollars for jeans that weren't even comfortable.

"Let me have a shot at that spontaneity thing, Kerry," Randall said hastily when she emerged from the bathroom. His face, completely serious, glowed pink like a mood light. "Please allow me to offer you a drink, Kerry. Herbal tea? Hot chocolate?" He was still wearing his parka.

Flashing back on the horsehair couch, on the candle falling into the bath, on Randall's shadowy alarmed face, Kerry buried her wet head into his shoulder and laughed like a seal.

"I thought the seduction scene would come later," Randall explained when they were between the sheets of Randall's bed and eating the Chinese food they'd ordered in. "I had the seduction scene slotted for, say, three months from now."

"You had a *schedule?*"

"I'm glad I departed from it," he admitted, and they both laughed.

Kerry traced his profile with her finger, ran her foot down his calf.

"I may not be, in every respect, the brightest guy on the block," Randall said, turning to her again. "Can you overlook that in a man?"

•   •   •

"Voilà! My *pièce de résistance!"* Randall said, somewhat out of breath from the stairs. He put down his box of photographs, pulled out the end one, held it out to Kerry. The photograph showed a blue ball floating within the skeleton of a yellow cube. Dice, balls, dominoes and blocks surrounded the cube, some of the objects seeming to float in mid-air while others did not. "This deserves to be the focal point of my exhibition, Kerry, don't you think?"

Kerry looked up from the boiling water she was pouring into a glass coffee pot.

"Now, that's interesting," she said carefully, for she'd decided some time ago to stop being *nice*. Okay, so she was nice. But not *that* nice! Why couldn't she say what she really thought? About Randall's photography. In the bedroom. At work. At weddings (especially her own). In *life*!

Mostly, though, inside her own head. (Step one, she sometimes coached herself: stop being so goddamned *nice*!)

She was not, for example, entirely the *babe* that Randall seemed to think she was. She had a child, for one thing. Sometimes she didn't think Randall entirely got that.

"It's more complex than my other pieces, don't you think? There's more happening. The objects here, here and here are floating, aren't they?" Randall pointed to a die, a domino, a child's alphabet block. "Do you see they're floating?"

"Not the alphabet block. The alphabet block is resting on the mirror."

"Really? It looks that way?" Randall held the picture at arm's length and squinted sideways at it. "No! The alphabet block is floating!"

"It doesn't have to float, Randall. The picture is just fine even if the alphabet block doesn't float. It's fine, Randall. Lots of people will like these photos. Children might like these photos."

"Not Mackenzie."

Mackenzie, it was true, refused to look at Randall's pictures. She said they made her eyebrows hurt.

"In general, though. Mostly, I think children would like

them. I can see them on a wall in a children's bookstore."

"I can't get away from it." Randall shook his head as he placed his photograph back in the crate. "Everyone likes my old ones best. They like the floating nail. They like the cowboys and Indians. They even liked my wedding pictures. They like the ones that don't challenge me anymore."

"I'm a nurse, Randall," Kerry said, plunging the coffee. "I'm not trained to see things that aren't there." She poured two cups of coffee and handed one to Randall.

Randall was silent a few moments. "I might not be the best-known photographer out there," he said finally. "I might not be the most developed—"

"Or the thinnest," Kerry teased, sliding her hand between the buttons of his shirt and across his thickened middle.

"Hey. That's nice." He pressed her hand close. "Don't stop."

"Don't spill your coffee." She smiled, sliding her hand around to the side of his waist.

"Oh, damn!" Randall said, pulling away and looking at his watch. "Oh, damn! Oh, damn!"

"What's wrong?"

"Never mind," he said abruptly. "It's nothing." He rubbed his hand over his face. "It's just that I was going to tape a show on pyramids, but now Mackenzie is watching."

Kerry opened the fridge, returned the ground coffee to the freezer, shut the fridge with a barely audible smack. "Oh, well," she said. Her fingertips did a slow tango on the counter, then she lifted her chin brightly. "Mackenzie and I are more important than those old pyramids. Aren't we?"

"You are," Randall agreed unhappily. "You are." He reached down and popped one bubble on the edge of the bubble wrap. "I just thought I might get some ideas from the pyramids. That's all."

• • •

"The bed smells funny," Mackenzie said. She lay in the very centre of the bed in Randall's spare room, her greying baby blanket heaped on the pillow beside her head, her arms and legs straight down, like a clothespin doll.

"It's just the sheets," Kerry answered, leaning over to smell the pillowcase. "Randall dries them on the drying rack, and we dry our sheets in the dryer." She rubbed her finger along Mackenzie's hairline. "Baby hair," she murmured, inviting her into an old game. "I can still see your baby hair."

But Mackenzie wasn't in the mood for that game. Her marshmallow mommy had gone hard and shiny. She was different when Randall was there, set apart, unreachable, like a crinkly-wrapped present she was forbidden to open.

Her mother straightened the bedcover, tucked in the already tucked-in sheets. "Wasn't it nice of Randall to buy you this bed, sweetie?" Her voice was a bright telephone voice. "Remember how he asked and I said you'd like white? Randall wants you to be cozy, sweetheart."

Mackenzie pulled her ragged blanket under the sheet with her, then pressed her hand into Kerry's. "I like my own bed," she said. She clamped her other hand onto the edge of Kerry's sweater, gnawed her lip as she looked at the sharp-cornered furniture, at the worried man-in-the-moon face made by the knobs of the plywood dresser, at her mother, who looked shellacked, shiny, sealed away. "I like my own bed in my own house."

• • •

Kerry was already in bed when Randall stepped out of the shower.

"Depth of field," he said, sliding down under the sheets and wrapping his arms around her. He was naked, except for his glasses, and his chest hair was still slightly damp from the shower. "Depth of field. There I was, a dumb old bachelor. Dumb but happy. Just me, my lenses, my filters, my lights and my mirrors. Then you came," he continued, sliding his hand down her spine, "and I didn't have to do anything. I just increased my depth of field by stopping down the lens, and there you were, just *there* in my life."

Sometimes, between visits, with so many other things going on, Kerry lost track of what mattered. But now that she was here with Randall, she remembered. Her skin remembered, or some dumb knowing just outside her skin. A fraction of a moment before their skins met, she remembered.

This darkness, this density between them, this—*this*—is what mattered.

"You didn't kiss me!" It was a voice from somewhere else, from some other place, from the other bedroom down Randall's darkened hallway.

Kerry remained motionless.

"You didn't kiss me!" The voice was more insistent.

Kerry pushed herself up on one elbow, pulling herself out of the dark web where she was lodged. She turned her face in the direction of the voice. "I did, sweetie!" she called, her voice disembodied and cheerful. She looked at the greenish glow of the street light through the sheet Randall had thumb-tacked over the window.

"You *didn't*!" the voice trailed back through the darkness.

"Don't go," Randall said, pulling Kerry close. "She has to learn."

"My kiss!" The fish hook trolled the darkness again. "I didn't get my kiss!"

"Kerry," Randall said, cautioning her. His arms tightened around her.

There was a sharp intake of breath, hers then his. From far away there came the mosquito whine of a police siren.

"But I always go," Kerry said. "I *have* to go, Randall. I can't suddenly *not* go now."

She waited for him to say something, but when he didn't, she slid out of his arms, felt with her feet for her slippers.

Mackenzie, bustling and happy now that she had her

mother, needed her blanket straightened. She needed her pillow fluffed. She needed a fresh glass of water because a spider had been drinking from this one.

Kerry hummed a little, massaged Mackenzie's back, trying not to throw things off by hurrying too little or too much. Finally, when the air felt still, she tiptoed back through the clammy darkness to Randall's room. She stepped out of her slippers, pulled herself back into the warmth of Randall's orbit.

"Hi there, good-looking," she whispered into his neck, settling herself around his warm back and legs.

His only response was a light, rasping snore.

"Randall!" she whispered, rocking his shoulder. "Randall?"

He rolled over onto his back, pulled her close, but continued breathing deeply and evenly.

Darkness sifted down through her like soot, darkening her blood, lodging in her bones. She tried to pull Randall's roughened sheet over her shoulder, tried to relax in his embrace.

"Randall? Are you awake?" She tried to find a comfortable position between his collarbone and his surprisingly bony shoulder. "Randall, I'm cold." She *was* cold. Why was it, she asked herself, that she was so often cold in Randall's house?

She ducked out of his reaching arms, then pulled open his top dresser drawer, making as much noise as she decently could. She pulled on a woolly pair of Randall's socks, pulled open another drawer, helped herself to one of his sweat-shirts.

She was completely awake now and far too miserable to sleep. She made her way down the unlit stairs and into the kitchen, where she heated milk in the microwave. Where was the cocoa? She opened the cupboard, the fridge, the freezer.

Randall's freezer was an icy archive, everything in same-sized Tupperware containers and labelled on the end. MASHED POTATOES. MASHED POTATOES. MASHED POTATOES. Then, a more complicated label: TOY SOLDIERS / BLOCKS / DICE.

She opened the corner of the container to find several zip-lock bags filled with what appeared to be negatives. She replaced the container. KEWPIE DOLLS / PLASTIC DUCKS / COWBOYS AND INDIANS, read another. Then, at the bottom of the third stack, WEDDING PICTURES.

Wedding Pictures.

She slid that container out, placed it on the kitchen table, sat down and opened one of the zip-lock bags. She slipped one cool strip of negatives from its sleeve, held it up to the light.

She saw a tiny black bride, feathered, plumed, splayed out and pinned to the brown-black sky like an exotic moth, the tiny white groom, male of the species, pinned to the sky beside her. The next negative showed a dusty purple-skinned bride and a pink and white groom cutting a cake. In another, the ornate dark female approached the male across the pale candied rainbow.

Was that her and Gordon? No, the bridal headpiece didn't seem right—but it might have been. The black and the white, the male and the female, the yin and the yang. The heart-breaking hopes and the maimed intentions. The male was taller but somehow the less substantial-looking of the species. The female, large and dark, purple-skinned, was more dense, more elaborate, more vast and unknowable.

So many brides! So many bridegrooms! What had become of them? Maybe everything had worked out perfectly for them. Maybe, with the colours reversed to the everyday, with costumes pushed to the back of closets, with rainbows and latticed footbridges replaced by toasters and refrigerators, they had gone on to live happily and honourably with each other. It was possible. Some people did that.

Kerry registered a sound from upstairs, a sound, it seemed to her now, that had actually begun a few moments before. A squeaking or a mewing. She listened again. The negatives shone black under the lamplight.

More mewing. Was someone crying? She pushed herself back from the negatives, hearing feet now, thudding across the floor above her head.

"Mackenzie!" she called in a hushed voice. She ran up the narrow, darkened stairs. "Mackenzie!"

But on the landing, it was Randall who collided with her. Randall with a sheet bath-towelled around him. Wordlessly, he pulled her into his sheet and pressed her open hand to the centre of his chest. He was breathing hard, his skin was slicked with sweat and his heart pounded against the palm of her hand. He smelled of soap, sleep, anise.

"I woke up," he said, his voice raw and broken open, as though still inside a bad dream. "I woke up and I thought you were gone." His breath warmed the back of her neck. "Don't leave me, Kerry. Promise me. Say you'll never leave me."

"I'm here, Randall." Kerry pressed her face into his shoulder. "I'm here." How glad she was that he'd woken and come for her, how right it felt to be here in his arms. She held him while his breath steadied, while she warmed herself at his furnace.

Then, slowly, somewhere within the circle of their embrace, Kerry became aware of the slightest trembling. She waited for the tremor to stop, but it continued, through their breathing, through their united heartbeat, through their slow rhythmic rocking, a tiny panicked wingbeat, a racing pulse, some small frenetic fluttering.

Was it Randall who was shaking? Was it some peculiar tic of their combined muscles and nerves? Was it early morning traffic, or maybe some huge machine boring down into slabs of rock deep inside the earth?

Or am I the one shaking? Kerry asked herself. Could it be me? (Step one, she told herself, reciting her new mantra: stop being so goddamned *nice*.)

She sensed the three-point constellation of them in the darkness—she and Randall, two orange stars here together, Mackenzie, a blue star above and to the side. It was large, what Randall asked her, and large how she answered.

And so she was trembling. She was frightened—it was true—but didn't she have the right? Here she was, on this darkened landing, here in this man's arms, here—*here!*—in her life.

people like **us**

Paula's son, Matt, is doing well now—real job, serious girl-friend—and he is back from Woolamaroo, Australia, for a visit.

"Okay! That's it!" he says, slamming his hand down on the dash. "Open the trunk, I'll get my bags and I'm out of here."

"What? *Here?*" Paula turns to him from behind the steering wheel, ice scraper in hand, powdery ice scrapings dusting her Day-Glo orange mitts. The grey banks of snow on the side of the road are littered with snow removal signs, and a single anti-war placard that reads *No Blood for Oil*. Cars in the oncoming lane plough past, dragging clouds of wintery exhaust. "But we're not even home yet. Why do you want to get out here?"

"I can see I'm not welcome," Matt says.

"But you *are* welcome. Of course you're welcome. I've been *waiting* for you to come."

This is true. She has been waiting. While she's been waiting, she's been considering replacing her good silverware with less pawnable hardware store cutlery. While she's been waiting, she's moved her best jewellery from the retired butter dish, where she normally keeps it, to the bottom of her underwear drawer, where she's pretty sure he would be unwilling to venture. ("Gross!" he used to yell if her laundry so much as shared the same dryer as his.) While she's been waiting, she's made a pumpkin pie, one of his favourites, then reduced it to a small black meteorite in the oven. But she has been waiting all the same.

She is still not used to her weedy, six-foot-tall teenage son with his baggy dark clothes and his size twelve Nikes transformed now into this bulky grown man with a three-quarter-length dress coat, brown leather oxfords and—most shocking of all—very fine lines scooping out furrows underneath his eyes. His hair, always blond, is a dyed blond now, the roots fashionably dark, like the shadows on his chin and cheeks.

"I tell a joke and you don't even laugh," this deep-voiced stranger accuses. "You don't even smile."

A UPS truck passes, heaving dirty slush against the windshield, and the wipers flap wildly this way and that, much like her own heart, which is likewise flinging off sleet and ice as best it can.

"Let's talk at home," Paula says, scraping again at the inside of the windshield while she manoeuvres the car along the road. The defrost throws up air, but air that's only somewhat warm, not hot enough to seriously discourage the frost that keeps creeping back into the porthole she's scraped for herself.

"All I said was, there was where me and Dustin had the cops after us and we crawled up on the girders under the bridge and they drove right under us. Dustin's mom laughs about all that now. She laughs about that time you and her were called down to the police station and I called that blond cop Goldilocks."

"But I don't find it funny. Why should I laugh?"

"See? There you go again," Matt bellows, his bulky shoulders contained by the seat belt but lunging briefly in her direction, his face puffed up in anger. He fills up his half of her Toyota, his head almost touching the ceiling. "You never let up, do you? We were kids, okay? *Okay?*" He jabs his newly pudgy forefinger in her direction. "We were *kids*!"

"I know. I was there. Remember?"

"Okay, that's it. That's *really* it." He explodes against the side door, a cumbersome jack-in-the-box, and for a moment Paula is not sure what's happening. "Pull over *right there* and open the trunk." He is pointing to a gravelly stretch of polar ice in front of a Lebanese butcher shop, barely visible between grimy heaps of snow. "I guarantee you'll never see or hear from me again. *Here!* Pull over right *here*!"

She pulls over as close as she can get, blocking traffic behind, battling with the temptation to take him at his word and simply let him go, while he—face set—fumbles furiously with his seat belt, jerks at the levers on the door.

"Come on, Matt," Paula says, reaching over to press her hand over his. "You spent all that money to come. You used up your holiday days. Come on, Matt. I want you to stay."

His knuckly hand twists away from hers, a belligerent tomcat who won't be tamed. The vehicle behind blares its horn, flashes its massive headlights. Paula rolls down her window and flails her arm in a circle, signalling for them to drive around, but the truck only revs its engine and lets loose with another mastodon bellow.

"Please stay, Matt."

He stares straight ahead, face lined, cheeks jowly. He's travelled eight hours by bus to Sydney, then has been cramped into an economy airline seat for twenty-six more hours, not counting stopovers or the required passage through customs in Honolulu and Vancouver. It is February, when Australia is at the beach and airfares to Canada are most affordable.

He drops his head forward and rubs the space between his eyebrows with his thumbs. "Okay," he says very quietly. He rights himself, leans his head back against the headrest, opens his eyes. "O-*kay*!" He rotates his huge ungloved hands in the air, gesturing for her to drive.

She drives, ducking down to see out of the cleared space on the window, pressing her mitt to the left side of her face. Ten days, she tells herself. Nine after today, eight if they take away the day of departure. And surely he will spend a day or two with his dad.

As long as he doesn't get up to his old tricks. The drugs,

the alcohol, the god knows what. Helping himself to the money in her wallet, pawning her camera.

Turning into her street, she thinks of another worry, one that lies in the opposite direction but which is no less valid. As long as the comforts of home don't undo him (as they have at least once before), leaving him collapsed on her couch, watching videos, living on Froot Loops and pizza, unwilling or unable to face the world.

"Why is it so goddamned *cold*?" Matt says, pulling his light coat tightly around his bulky shoulders.

"It's February," Paula answers, smiling over at him as best she can. "February in Ottawa, remember?"

•   •   •

"Five hundred dollars," Matt says at home, hanging his coat on a hanger and holding it out for his mother to see. Paula watches him straighten the shoulders, smooth down the wrinkles, brush vigorously at an invisible fleck of lint on the sleeve.

She takes the travel-creased coat to a lamp in the living room, runs her hand over the fabric, examines the collar and the bound buttonholes. He wore a coat similar to this when he was about eight, one of hers. Only then, he had safety-pinned numerous pockets into the inside, emulating his hero, Inspector Gadget.

"Cashmere," she says, smiling across at him. "Such nice clean lines. This is a beautiful coat, Matt."

"Some guys don't care what they wear," he explains in his rumbly voice, as serious and authoritative as if he were discussing prospects for peace on the evening news. "They'll wear an old raincoat or a windbreaker to work. But I like to dress well. I like to wear a suit and a coat. I feel better, and it doesn't cost that much more."

"You're right. A coat like that is going to last you a long time," Paula says. Then she flops forward to laugh into the coat on her lap.

"What's so funny? *What?*"

"It's just that the last time I saw you, you were wearing those baggy black sweatshirts. And those pants that dragged on the ground."

"Yeah. Well," he says. He looks pleased, though, takes the coat from her, checks it over again, hangs it in the hall closet. "I'm a high roller like you. I get it from you, Mom."

"From me?"

"Yeah. Look at it." He flings an open suitcase onto her favourite reading chair, then sweeps his hand around the room. "Couches and coffee tables and those old antique lamps and shit. You got yourself your oriental rug, your bird pictures on the wall."

"I guess."

"No kidding, Mom." He is dragging a coffee table to the couch, plugging in a laptop computer as he speaks. "Whenever I see those grey-haired backpacking types with jumbled-up clothes and covered in peace pins, I know—surprise—

they're probably not as totally whacked out as they look. They probably pay their electricity bill same as the next guy, they probably have a roof over their heads to store all those— yummy-yummy—whole grains and lentils. Whenever I see that type, I think, 'Yup. That's my mom.'"

Paula laughs out loud again. "So you have that type in Australia too?"

But his fingers are already flying over the keyboard, and he is pointing to the screen, showing her pictures of work and of his girlfriend, My-Lee, pictures of his pet boa constrictor, snapshots from the celebration for the Most Valuable Employee award, which made this trip possible.

"That's the actual *ocean*?" Paula asks, not really prepared for any of this, though he's been sending her postcard-like pictures by email. "Palm trees? They're not *plastic*, are they? Where'd you get this stuff? My-Lee's so pretty! How big is that snake going to get?"

He's already sending messages back, explaining at the same time and all in a jumble about the people at work, about My-Lee's Vietnamese family, about how he endeared himself to her grandfather by eating a dish containing pigeon heads, about his now-favourite lunch, whitebait, about his boss who took him on a carnival ride that involved dropping twelve floors down an elevator shaft in a glass box.

So it's real, Paula thinks, hugging herself with the oven mitts in the kitchen. She pulls a roast chicken out of the oven, then stares at her reflection in the window, her grey-haired

troll self floating out across the city sky like a Woody Allen
mother. It's real. The job, the girlfriend, the flat he shares
with three young men on the other side of the world.

Not that she has doubted him.

Still.

"Why do you keep saying I *rent out cars?*" Matt demands,
outraged, his elbows on the table, an overcooked drumstick
in his hands. "*Rent out cars?* I don't fucking *rent* out *cars*!" He
throws down the bone like King Henry the Eighth, his teeth
enamel white, his mouth greasy. "*I am an assistant manager of
the largest vehicle leasing and rental agency in the larger Woolamaroo area!*" He wipes his hands on something, his pants or
the edge of the tablecloth, then reaches across the table for
the other drumstick. "We serve the whole southeast coast.
We got a budget of nine million, a fleet of two hundred
and fifty vehicles, a clientele, for the most part, of business
people and German tourists. I'm the only one who can make
the Germans laugh. *Guten Tag, Fräulein! Ihre Augen sind blau
wie das Meer!* I tell them their eyes are as blue as the goddamned ocean. They love it. They lap it up."

"Really? Isn't that wonderful!" she keeps saying. "Here,
Matt. Did you try the stuffing? You love this kind of stuffing."

Matt drops his gaze to the stuffing for a full half minute,
then, very deliberately, lifts his arm to the table and swings it
sideways, sweeping his plate and cutlery to the side. He looks
up, all expansiveness gone, locks eyes with his mother.

"Why didn't you visit me in juvie?" he says, the muscles in his jaw tightening, his face hardening.

"Pardon?"

"You heard me. Why didn't you visit me in juvie?"

There is an unnatural stillness in the room, as if the power's been cut off.

"But I did visit you. I remember visiting you there."

"Not on Thanksgiving. You didn't visit me on Thanksgiving."

Everything from those days is buried beneath six feet of ice in Paula's mind. Strangers appearing at the door, some of them blank-faced men with expensive cars idling at the curb, others dressed in American ghetto-style clothing, sometimes walking straight in without knocking. There was much selling of CDs going on. CDs and stamps from Matt's childhood stamp collection, which he apparently advertised on the Internet. ("Look. See? CDs. *Okay?* Stamps. *All right?*" he said, flashing CDs or packets of stamps before her eyes.)

At first she believed him. Then she didn't. She didn't know what she believed or what she didn't believe anymore.

By then Gavin, Paula's husband and Matt's father, was disappearing by increasingly rapid increments to a job in the Arctic, where it appeared he was involved with a young woman named Brandy. (Brandy? Brandy! They'd not so long ago had a part Labrador retriever named Brandy whom they'd had to put down due to a skin disease!)

Sometimes Gavin came back to Ottawa for meetings, occasionally showing up at the house, ostensibly to see Matt, but also, it seemed, to inquire whether his current hairstyle made him look younger. He'd taken to wearing brightly coloured bandanas to conceal (or possibly highlight) the scratches he sometimes had down his neck, once down the side of his face. He bore these wounds with slightly distracted pride, as though they were decorations from a distant, almost mythical war.

Paula explained about Gavin's absence to Matt's school counsellors and vice-principals, on the lookout for a mentor, hoping for a turnaround, petitioning for yet another chance, very likely spending more time in school than Matt.

At home, she began to wander about the house with a glass of Scotch permanently glued to the palm of her hand.

"Has anyone seen Gavin?" she liked to ask. She checked behind cushions and in the linty pockets of her bathrobe, the ice dispenser providing a raucous and reliable laugh line. "Oh dear, I do believe I've mislaid Gavin!"

For the most part, Matt and his friend, Dustin, gave up the pretence of school altogether. They took to hanging out in the local tot lot, their baggy pants and hooded sweatshirts making them look like larger, more ominous versions of the toddlers brought there by their sitters. Matt and Dustin liked to suck on candy in the shape of baby bottles or infant pacifiers. Sometimes this candy was attached to their sweatshirts with safety pins, other times it dangled on cords about their necks.

One afternoon they looked down from their perch on the blue dinosaur-shaped climber to see two police officers approaching them from different sides of the playground. They threw their scales and drugs to the ground and ran, but the string from Matt's pacifier-shaped candy snagged on the chain-link fence and he was arrested.

His belligerence toward the police didn't help. His unwillingness to co-operate by naming Dustin didn't help. What probably helped least of all was the prescription bottle bearing Matt's name, address and phone number, originally containing medication for an ear infection and now containing street drugs. Matt was tried in court and sentenced to four months in the juvenile detention centre.

"This other guy's mother brought in a whole Thanksgiving dinner, turkey, gravy, stuffing, the works," Matt tells Paula now. "I waited all afternoon in that puke-coloured lounge. There was a big guy hogging the TV and breathing barf in my face, but I couldn't do dick! There was fucking *blood* on the walls! I waited, but they didn't call my name."

"You could bring food in?" All that comes to Paula's mind now is a cartoon picture of a layer cake, a cherry on top, a file comically concealed inside it.

"You knew. There was a whole leaflet about it. You said you'd make a Thanksgiving dinner and bring it in. Then you didn't even show."

"I said I would?" Paula reaches down into the stale laundry hamper of her brain for this information, but comes up empty-handed. She stares at him, shaking her shaggy grey head. "I don't remember. I don't know what happened."

"*I* know. How come it's such a big mystery to *you*? I know what you were doing. You were hammered. You were pouring it back and making jokes into the mirror. You didn't give a fuck about me or how I was doing. As long as *you* were having a good time, that's all *you* cared."

Later, when she is scrubbing the roasting pan, she hears Matt tapping numbers into the phone, calling Dustin and other people he'd gone to school with. "G'day mate!" he says again and again, his voice jovial but quick and high-pitched with nervousness.

"Daniel's in Toronto, Mitch is in Argentina with his dad, and Dustin's being a dickhead like usual," he reports.

Paula has heard about Dustin, that he too has turned a new leaf and is doing an honours degree in classics at university.

"I take the rap for him and now he's too busy to see me."

"I found your skates," Paula says, her hands still in the sink, but nodding toward his old hockey skates that she's placed on a newspaper under the kitchen table. "We could go skating on the river. It's really neat. People make paths every which way. It's like a maze."

"You go ahead, Mom. I'll let you know if I'm in the mood to drown in fifty-below water."

"There's something at the museum I want to see. And then—hey!—there's your dad," she adds more enthusiastically, remembering. She wrings out the dishrag as briskly as if she were wringing a chicken's neck. "Are you going to call your dad, Matt?" (Let Gavin take the flak for a while.)

"Call my *sad*? Call my *bad*? Call my *had*? Oh, call my *daaaad*. Why didn't you say so in the first place?"

• • •

She calls Gavin at work while Matt's still sleeping.

"I know he's there," Gavin says. She can hear him tapping away on his computer. "He called me yesterday."

"He's really different. You should see him. He's so proud of his job." Once she asked Gavin how he could talk and work at the same time, and he said he checked his email while he talked to her. "And the award—that's a *huge* deal. Can you give him the money to go up and see you for a couple of days?"

"I offered him my points to come up, but he didn't want to come."

"You *did*?" (tap tap tap) "He *didn't*?" (tap tap tap) "Well, are you coming out this way? Don't you have meetings or something? It would be such a shame if he didn't see you."

"He can come here if he wants to see me."

"But he's come all this way."

"Stop spoon-feeding him. Let him *reach* for something. Let him . . ."—and Paula realizes the typing has stopped— "let him . . . *desire* . . . something."

Gavin's almost-whispered word, *desire*, lies awkward as a flopping fish on the vast table of Arctic air between them.

•   •   •

"You want to know the worst thing I ever did, Mom?" They're driving back from the discount store where they've bought Matt a winter parka, mitts and toque.

"No, Matt, I don't. I really don't. That's the kind of thing that it's better for me not to know." A tiny drumbeat of panic, with its attendant echo of anticipatory grief, starts up in her, though, and prickly with sudden anxiety Paula tugs at her scarf, pulls off her woolly hat.

They've been taking a meandering route home, past the house they lived in when Matt was small, past the old hockey rink, past the old tobogganing hill, taken over now by a row of upscale condominiums, past the school where Matt started a fire in a Dumpster in grade four.

"But I want to tell you, Mom. I drank the communion wine from that church." With a sideways nod of his head, Matt indicates a large stone church with stained glass windows.

"That one?" Paula slows down in front of the church, then pulls over to the curb. She leans over Matt to get a better look at it.

Matt screws his mouth around to the side, bites at the inside of his lip. "You know when I told you I was at a sleepover at a church with that boy named Kevin? We wrote down false names. Then, when everyone was playing these dorky games, we snuck into the back and drank the wine." He stares out at the church, turning his head slowly from side to side, rubbing the bristles on his chin over his knuckles.

"That's not so bad, Matt," Paula says quietly. "That's a kid kind of thing to do."

"It is?" Matt turns around to stare at her.

"When we were kids, we drank all the pickle juice from our church kitchen and left the pickles sitting dry in their jars. That was our big adventure."

"You did that?"

"If that's the worst thing you ever do, then, well . . . there's hope, right?"

"Some old geezer came charging in and started hollering at us. 'You boys come with me! I'm going to call your parents!' So we took off through the church and I threw the bottle through that stained glass window."

Paula stares at his silhouette in the darkened car. She remembers now seeing the boarded-up window. She remembers reading about the vandalism in the paper. "*You* did that?" she says, drawing back. "But why? Why would you do something like that?"

"See? See? I *knew* you'd have a hairy!" he shouts. "I knew you'd be like that! You were always that way. You would never *talk* to me. You would never just *talk*. Do you know how fucking *awful* it was, having a mother like you?"

She pulls out into traffic and continues driving, quickly now, toward home. "I did *so* talk to you. I tried to. Remember all those times we went driving like this? That was so I could talk to you."

"See? See?" he says, pointing his finger at her. "So *you* could talk. So *you* could talk. But what about *me*? Did *I* get a chance to talk? Did you ever listen to what *I* had to say?"

"Didn't I?"

"It was always just like now, why'd you do this, why didn't you do that. You never took my side. You never saw it my way."

"But I'm your mother—"

"My mother! My mother!" he hollers. "I wish I'd died on an *abortionist's table* rather than have you as my mother!"

"Jesus, Matt." Paula hunches down lower over the wheel, her chest registering a shock, as if slammed by a ball she didn't see coming. She should have seen it coming, though. She's heard this before.

"No one," he continues, more quietly now, "ever *really* talked to me. No one sat me down at the table and said, 'So, how's your life going, son?' No one ever did that. Not one person."

She pulls into their driveway, turns off the ignition and sits perfectly still for a moment before taking the key out.

"Did you?" He is starting to raise his voice again. "Even once? Once?"

"No," she says curtly. "I never said exactly that."

Inside the house, she hears him talking about schedules and upgrades to someone from Air Canada.

"Matt?" she says, picking up the extension. "What's going on?"

"I'm getting an earlier flight," he says. "My business here is done. *Finito*. I'm ready to go."

"Let's not part on a bad footing, Matt. Let's try to make something positive out of this. Who knows when we'll see each other again?"

"Sir?" the Air Canada woman says. "Sir?"

"Okay," he says at last. He sounds infinitely weary. "I'll stay."

• • •

She wakes to hear Matt talking quietly to someone, and after some time realizes he is talking to his girlfriend, My-Lee, a quiet, almost inaudible murmur, neither of them seeming to have much to say but seeming to want to stay on the phone anyway.

It's been so long since she's been in a conversation like that. She realizes she's almost forgotten about conversations like that. Her conversations with her friends now are relentlessly chatty, filled with wisecracks, bristling with cheer. They've become shrill, she supposes, in their middle-aged eagerness to throw back their heads and laugh. In their determination to have fun. (Would the world be too unbearably sad if they stopped laughing for five minutes?)

She remembers going home on the bus from an anti-war demonstration at the Parliament Buildings and recognizing the young man on the seat beside her as someone she'd spoken to at the march.

"Maybe it does some good, anyway." She found herself speaking in a jolly older-person-to-younger-person voice. "Even if George Bush didn't see us." She was echoing a sentiment circulated at the demonstration, disappointed as they were not to have had George Bush witness their presence.

The young man, who was wearing glasses and a Peruvian hat with earflaps, looked at her a moment, then smiled shyly. "It gives me hope," he said. A simple, stripped-down voice.

Why was it so hard to speak in that simple, stripped-down way?

It gives me hope.

She gets up for a glass of water, then sits down in the dark living room where Matt is talking. Matt hands the phone to her.

"Hello?" she says into the receiver.

"Paula? This is My-Lee." A forceful, almost boisterous, twangy voice. Paula moves the receiver a bit away from her ear, pictures a large, athletic woman on horseback, galloping across the Pampas.

But no. Wrong continent. And from Matt's photos, she knows My-Lee is tiny.

"What time is it there?" Paula asks.

"I've just come home from work"—*weuk*—"and I'm relaxing"—*relexing*—"on the back deck."

"Can you see any of those little parrots with red vests?"

"I beg your pardon?" My-Lee laughs. "Say that again. But slower"—*sleuer*—"this time."

"Parrots? The ones with the red vests? Matt told me you have them in your backyard."

Matt grabs the phone from her hands, laughing. "Little parrots with red vests! My mom is asking about little parrots in red vests! The rainbow lorikeets? She's seriously nuts! I warned you about her, didn't I? Her brains are fried from too much broccoli!" Still laughing into the phone, he speaks now to Paula in a coddling way. "The birdies with the red vests have gone night-night, Mumsies. The birdies with the red vests will come out again in the morning-time."

She can make out the glint of his huge pleased smile in the darkness.

•   •   •

"Isn't this cute," Paula says. "The streets have historical names—Copernicus, Louis Pasteur. Is that because this is a university campus?"

Dustin has relented and agreed to see Matt, and Paula is driving Matt to Dustin's university residence. Matt is wearing his good cashmere coat and is freshly shaved, smelling of his favourite aftershave, Preferred Stock, which he bought just today, and in quantity, for it is not available in Australia.

"Copernicus? Historical? What are you talking about?" Matt says.

"Wasn't he the one, you know, who thought the earth went around the sun?"

"Copernicus? Copernicus? Copernicus is a kind of pizza. *Duh.*"

So school really did wash right over him, Paula thinks as she drives down the ruts of the snow-narrowed street.

Well, fine.

Excellent, in fact. All that forced inactivity, all those papers worn thin by erasing, all those meetings and blamings and testings. All that misery down the tube. Good riddance to all of it.

My son has managed just fine without it, she says silently to the teachers, the psychologists, his grade three principal, whose standard greeting to Paula seemed to be, "Bad news, I'm afraid."

My son is the assistant manager of the largest vehicle leasing and rental agency in Woolamaroo, Australia!

"You know, when you were little, you were so smart. So curious," Paula says, glancing at Matt's profile, not sure if she should be saying what she is about to say. "You always had a frog or a cricket. Then, well . . . school. But you seem smart again to me now."

"I know," he says, turning to her, a look of surprise on his face.

"Why, do you think? Is it My-Lee?"

"Yeah, I guess." He presses his palm to his forehead. "But it's like my brain works better there. You know the way I used to sleep all day and stay up all night? Over there, I sleep at night and get up in the daytime."

"That's so good."

"It's because Australia's on the other side of the world," he explains, still serious, but turning the rear-view mirror toward himself. He runs his hands through his hair, checking from one side, then the other. "It's because the days and nights are reversed."

By the time she gets home, having stopped for groceries on the way, Matt is back.

"He told me I would have nothing in common," Matt says bitterly. "That's what he told me. Dustin. Can you believe it? We were already heading out to the pub with a bunch of guys from his floor. *Nothing in common!*"

Paula stares at him through the forest of packaged spaghetti, celery and French bread sticking up from her bag of groceries.

"I take the rap for him and now I got *nothing in common!*" He slams his fist again and again into a cushion, then looks up at Paula. "And it's not like *you* care."

"What about your dad? Are you going to go up and see your dad?" She puts down the groceries, pulls off her hat and boots.

Matt heaves the cushion to the floor, drops his head into his hands. "Nah. Brandy's there. It's too weird."

"That she's so young?"

"I don't know. You stick your hand into the fridge for milk and hit roses." He pulls his shoulders up around his ears and shivers. "It's creepy."

"Roses?" Paula says. Something inside her chest, possibly a lung, stands up, turns around, then drops down again.

"They got roses everywhere. Even on the goddamned toilet. And there's this incense burning." He pinches the bridge of his nose and coughs a little. "I'm allergic to all that incense shit."

Paula's lungs have begun to work again, but now the problem is with her eyes. Why are her eyes stinging? She's astonished by this herself. Gavin's been gone for *years* now.

She walks rapidly through the living room, picking up dirty dishes, pizza boxes and soft drink cans, not bothering to stand upright between one item and the next but remaining stooped for her entire sweep.

But Gavin had always been strictly a complimentary-hotel-soap man! she finds herself thinking as she sorts the cardboard, the glass and the cans into the recycling tubs in the porch. He travelled a lot for his job and always gave her complimentary hotel soaps for birthdays, Christmases, anniversaries. Sometimes, Paula remembers, there had also been a little shoe polishing cloth.

"What the fuck! What the *fuck!*" she hears Matt shouting.

She gets back to the living room in time to see Matt throwing the coat he's worn home to the floor. He steps on the hem and rips the coat down the back.

"This isn't even my coat! It's not *my fucking coat!* Someone took my coat and left me with their crummy Salvation Army coat!"

"But why *rip* it?" Paula stares at him, her mouth hanging open. "We could have taken it back. We can *still* go back. It's probably just an honest mistake."

"I'm not going back to a place where I have *nothing in common!*" Matt bellows, openly weeping now, water streaming down his face, kicking at the ruined coat on the floor. "I'm not ever going there! Don't you understand fucking *anything?* I'm not going back where I have *nothing in common!*"

•　•　•

"Where the hell are we?" Matt hisses into Paula's ear.

"The Bog People. Remember? I told you."

The museum room is dimly lit, barely illuminating various preserved corpses from the bogs of northern Europe. A sign explains that the lighting, which oscillates very slowly between dim and dimmer, is specially designed to prevent deterioration of the specimens.

"*What?*"

"The Bog People. They were buried in bogs thousands of years ago. Here, it explains." She touches a plaque on the wall, which displays a map of northern Europe marking the locations where various of the Bog People have been found. "It says they were preserved by the alkaline nature of the bog water."

One face looks collapsed down into itself, like a Halloween jack-o'-lantern left on the front steps a few months too long, but there is another of a young girl, eyes and hair reconstructed, a startled look, or possibly an impatient one, playing across her young face. In another barely illuminated exhibit just across lies a thin man, maybe fifty years old. Except for the coppery sheen of his skin, he looks as though he might simply have fallen asleep on a park bench a half-hour ago.

"Let's get out of here," Matt says, wheeling around, rearing up to look for an exit.

"But we just got here. It's interesting. Don't you find it interesting? See that man? Doesn't he remind you of someone? That nose and mouth? I know! Remember that Quaker man with the little mop dog who always fought with Brandy?"

"You're seriously, *seriously* sick," he says, louder now, looming over her in the semi-darkness. "Oh, shit." He clamps his elbow over his nose and mouth. "I can *smell* these things!"

"You *can't* smell them—"

"*I can smell them!*"

"Here," Paula says in a hushed voice. She pulls her change purse from her pocket, pulls a bill out of it. "Go have a coffee and a doughnut. I'll meet you in the cafeteria."

"I'm going to throw up!" Matt bellows back. "Can't you *hear* me? I'm going to *throw up* right here on the carpet!"

Instantly, security guards loom up around them, two on one side, two on the other. In the eerie half darkness, Paula sees one of them drawing something dark from his holster. A gun! she thinks, blanking out for a second. Then she sees the dark object is only a walkie-talkie.

"We're out of here!" Matt announces to startled onlookers. "If I wanted to see corpses, I'd go to a morgue!" He is already stalking ahead, glancing over his bulky shoulder to make sure she is following.

She has no one to blame but herself, Paula thinks as they make their way to the car park, Matt still thirty feet ahead. No one, of course, but Gavin.

And she does blame Gavin. She blames Gavin a lot. Weren't fathers supposed to show their sons how to *be* in the world? Weren't fathers supposed to model restraint and consideration? And all that self-serving slop about "desire"! Weren't fathers supposed to *desire* to see their children?

She pulls her keys out of her parka pocket with such force they flip around and smash painfully into the delicate bones and veins on the top of her hand. Almost instantly, her hand puffs up and goes purple.

She unlocks the car awkwardly with her left hand, manages to start the motor, then drives to the exit, her wounded hand on her lap. She pays the attendant, then turns the car homeward.

"So," says Matt, stretching out in the front seat, his arms behind his head. His voice is still slightly testy, but conversational now, a parody of the museum-attending son she wishes she had. "So. What did *you* like about it?"

"Like about it? *Like* about it? I didn't get to *see* it. How would I *know* what I *liked* or *didn't* like about it?"

"Don't start with me. I saw three corpses. You saw three corpses. What's so goddamned terrific about *three corpses*?"

Icy pellets hurl themselves kamikaze-style against the windshield as they pass over the bridge. Steam rises from the unfrozen section of the river below. Then, in the recently installed glass windows of the new War Museum, she sees ghostly images of themselves flicker past.

They're there. Then they're not.

"I don't know," she says at last. "I just find it interesting. That girl, for example. Maybe she was sewing a new dress. Or maybe she was in love with someone. They were people like us."

"You've got it all wrong." Matt jerks his seat bolt upright. "*Fuck*. You're so *totally* out of it."

"How?"

"We're *alive*! Or haven't you noticed that? *And they're fucking dead!* You don't see anything different about that? You *honestly* don't see anything *different* about that?" He stares at her, his face blank. "You got to get a life, Mom. Shit. You got to stop going around looking at dead people. Dye your hair. Put on some makeup. Go to a singles bar in Hull. Don't laugh, it would do you good." He watches her while she drives. "Dad's not coming back, Mom."

Paula turns to him, startled. "But I don't think about your father coming back."

She doesn't.

She has no *desire* (speaking of desire) to be reunited with Gavin.

But why, then, does she suddenly feel like Gretel, wandering about through a wintery forest? Hansel has absconded, it's true, with the fetching young witch. But that was ages ago, and she, Gretel, has a life. She goes to movies. She visits with her friends. She cycles, she skates. She works for the anti-war movement, most recently on a fundraiser involving the selling of Christmas trees.

Why, then, does she feel so desolate, so much on the edge of some sort of existentialist hypothermia?

When they reach the lantern-decorated streets of Chinatown, Matt climbs out. "I'm out of here," he announces, then slams the door, leaving her to drive home alone.

• • •

"I thought you should know," Gavin says on the phone. "Matt wants to go and I'm giving him my points."

Paula is propped up on the couch, wrapped in a comforter, her injured hand sandwiched between a cushion and a bag of frozen peas. "Your points to see you?" she asks.

"My points to go back to Australia."

"Without seeing you at all?"

"What?"

"But he's your *son*!"

"Loooook," Gavin says, uncoiling the word like a hastily thrown-up barrier against her. "He could use the points to come up here to see me, or he can use the points to upgrade and go back early. He wants to go back early. It's his decision. He's got a flight tomorrow morning at seven-fifteen."

Her hand, purple and lumpy and veined, looks like something quite separate from her. It looks like a purple cabbage forgotten at the back of a refrigerator, or maybe the hand of a bog person. Through her small side window she can see into her neighbour's now-illuminated side window. Sometimes in summer, through the screened windows, she's heard a woman cry out in pleasure. Another time she heard her neighbour sobbing long into the night.

Maybe Matt was right. Maybe she should go out more. Make an effort. Where would she begin? Should she get her colours done? That was something she'd never got around to doing in the old days. Did people still do that, get their colours done?

"I heard about the roses," she says.

Gavin doesn't answer, but she senses he's still on the line. In an unguarded moment he once complained to her about Brandy. "I can't talk to her the way I can talk to you." Paula tries to remember now what it was that she and Gavin had talked about. She turns the bag of peas over and places the colder side back on her hand again. How wooden cutting boards carried fewer germs than plastic cutting boards—that was one conversation.

"You didn't have money for Matt's hockey camp, but you have money to keep that place stocked in roses." She hears herself lay the words down like a tired old hand of cards.

"There you go, dragging up the past again," he answers in a quiet, skittish but almost companionable way.

"What colour of roses?" she inquires after a moment.

"Regular-coloured," he answers cagily.

Regular-coloured.

Regular-coloured roses!

.   .   .

"At least we made it to day five," she says to Matt when he comes in. She is still on the couch, her purpled hand still resting on a cushion on top of her comforter. "Let's give ourselves credit for that." The silverware has survived, as far as she knows. She hasn't noticed any money missing from her wallet. Strangers have not come to the door to make transactions of any kind. The police have not appeared. She and Matt were asked to remove themselves from the museum, it's true, but in the larger picture, that could surely pass for progress of a sort.

"Growth is never easy," Matt says, but in such a self-satisfied way she suspects he is thinking of her growth rather than his own. Still, this is not the kind of thing she's ever heard him say before, and she senses My-Lee's influences at work.

"Grab your parka. We're going skating," Matt announces, dropping her skates on the end of the couch and flashing his own in the air. "We got to get out and get some pictures."

"Ouch. What? *Now?* But you said the ice is too thin."

"It's all right." But he frowns down at her for a moment. "You go out there, right?"

"It's cold out, Matt. It's getting dark. We can get better pictures in here. Anyway, look at my hand. I can't do up laces."

He bends toward her hand, which is not as discoloured and swollen as before but which is arranged like a still life on the embroidered cushion.

"Eee-yooo!" he yells, making a face and jumping back. "Yuuuk!" He does a quick spastic dance of revulsion, then collects himself. "Never mind, Mom. You're all right. I'll do your laces for you. Come on. Let's go. We got to have ice! We got to have snow! Girls go for that kind of thing." Grinning, he pulls up the sleeve of his T-shirt and displays his flexed muscles. "Man! And the fucking elements!"

"A short skate," she says, pulling herself out of her comforter and standing up very slowly. By this time tomorrow, she reminds herself, he will be gone and she will be free to gather her wits in peace.

He waits impatiently, wearing reflective sunglasses, smelling of Preferred Stock, while she pulls on ski pants, a fleece jacket underneath her parka, a sheepskin hat, a double pair of mitts.

The sun has just disappeared below the horizon; there is almost no wind. The air smells of woodsmoke and is blue with cold. The river, when they get there, is streaked diagonally with mauve and grey, its paths, looping up and around, an elaborate bow of silver.

"You go out on the ice first," Matt says, suddenly wary again. "I can't afford to drown. I have a plane to catch tomorrow."

Paula pulls her sheepskin collar up against the cold. "My son from Australia," she says, or tries to say, to a man who is pushing a snow blower off the ice. The man, hunched into his parka and toque, can't hear her, but gives a nod.

"What's wrong with you?" Matt says. "Why are you doing that?"

"Doing what?"

"My s-s-son from Aus-t-t-tralia," he mimics her, lips flapping feebly, head crooked and a-tremble.

She drops her bundled self to the lawn chair, leaving the stump for Matt, and laces her skates as well and as quickly as she is able. He has forgotten his offer to help her with her laces and she is not going to ask. She is stung by his imitation of her. Surely she's not acting that way, so old and feeble. Though it is, in fact, exactly how she feels. A sled dog too spent to howl at the moon.

She stands and shoves herself quickly onto the ice, stumbling, but just for a moment. The ice is rough at the edges, but after that, hard, almost perfectly smooth, like antique glass.

She skates quickly and without looking back, wanting only to get away from him, taking first the path to the left, then another path veering off from that. The sky is pink-purple in the direction she is skating, the bridge black, laced tight with the golden ribbon of traffic across it.

Then there she is, in the exact centre of the bowl of the sky, with nothing but herself, cold air, sky and the silvery glide of her skates on the ice. Something like a bubble of light rises up inside her. The old thrill of feeling her skates cutting into the ice, of hearing the clatter of her blades clipping across the frozen river.

But what a *lot* of clatter, she finds herself thinking a moment later.

She looks down and sees the movement of a pair of dark skates winging along inches behind hers. She turns her head, but doesn't need to turn far. There is Matt's face, his mouth and nostrils steaming white, just behind her shoulder. He feels so close, he might, as in days past, be riding in her backpack.

She skates faster, and he skates faster.

She slows down, and he slows down.

She turns abruptly onto a narrower, breakaway path, then back to the main path, trying to dislodge him, but he follows close behind her again.

She skates along the wider ribbon of ice, then swerves trickily off onto a figure-eight loop, to see if she can shake him. But she can't get rid of him. He sticks close as a shadow.

She begins to calculate their combined weight in her head. She is not a small person, and neither is he. She hadn't anticipated both of them out here so close together. She glances down at the dark ice. What if the ice breaks? What if they go through? Would there be some sort of warning, or would they plunge straight down? (Will some other mother's son, a thousand years hence, be furious to have to gaze upon their preserved forms in a museum?)

He seems to think she can protect him. Protect him? What a notion! Her record of providing protection is imperfect. And besides, there are forces of nature at work here. If the ice were to break, what could she possibly do? She's not, after all, the kind of creature he read about when he was eight, the type with the ability to transform herself into any sort of thing, in this case an inflatable life raft.

She doesn't think they will go through, though. In one place, where the ice is clear except for bubbles, it looks a foot thick.

Suddenly, Matt shoves something dark, his camera, over her shoulder and into her face.

"You'll have to move back," she says, cutting the edge of her blades into the ice to stop. Her lips are stiff as cardboard in the cold. "Don't you want to see all of yourself in the picture? Don't you want it to show you skating?"

He moves back, but only a step.

"It's all right here," he says.

She takes off her mitts—it is impossible, for the moment, to favour her injured hand—holds up the camera and looks through the viewfinder. Then, quickly—for the bones in her hands are doing some kind of reverse combustion in the cold—she sees the head and shoulders of a grown man, large and dark and sombre, his sunglasses reflecting back two images of sky. A man she knows and doesn't know. A man she raised but who finds his home on the other side of the earth.

"Fuck," he says, slamming his gloved fists together in the cold. "Fuck. I'm freezing. *Just take it.*"

So she does. She takes it.

Then she skates with him to the side where they've left their boots.

She and this man who is her son.

ragtime

Edee had plenty of coats. She had a whole closet full of coats. She had her supply-teaching coat, for example, a navy wool coat with a double row of brass buttons. She had a quilted nylon coat. She had a red and black lumberman's jacket. She had the usual collection of parkas, anoraks, rain gear and wind shells. She even had a luxurious Persian lamb coat she'd bought at a thrift store.

The Persian lamb coat had a beautifully draped shawl collar, huge glass cat's eye buttons and a blue satin lining edged with a row of tiny folded satin points, enchanting as origami. On an inner pocket, Edee discovered hand-embroidered letters that spelled out her own given name—*Edith*—satin-stitched in elegant script-style letters, complete with loops, curlicues and a sprig of mauve lilacs. The coat was as intricately detailed as a tarot card, and seemed just as weighted with significance.

The Persian lamb coat was wonderfully heavy and wonderfully warm, but when Edee put it on at home, she was startled to see, looking back from her own mirror, an ash-coloured woman, older than she remembered, a woman of barely concealed weariness and disappointment. She looked, in this coat, as though she'd suffered, as if she'd pulled herself together as best she could and resigned herself to a life that was not of her own choosing.

"For the love of Pete," Edee said aloud.

She had to cover one eye and then the other before taking a deep breath and going on to check herself at other angles in the mirror.

Persian lamb coats were, strictly speaking, old ladies' coats, she finally decided as she slipped out of the coat and hung it in the very back of her hall closet. You likely had to be incredibly young or incredibly old to carry one off.

So when Edee's new (and not so very new) flame, Richard, asked her to a movie, she wore a short smart black wool jacket that set off her pewter hair to advantage. The jacket was cut on the bias and had a bit of a swing to it when she walked, which made her look good and feel good too.

The word was, as it happened, *sparkly*. It made her look sparkly.

Sparkliness was a quality Richard valued highly in her. Of course, Richard valued Edee just being Edee, and had said this on several occasions. But at other times, issuing an invitation to dinner, or suggesting a movie, he was likely to add,

"Bring your sparkly self." As if this lighter, more animated and less demanding self were as readily available as a can of peas on a shelf.

It was, in fact, the whole issue of sparkliness—or, more exactly, her lack of a reliable supply of said sparkliness—that had caused their relationship to founder, dissolve in mid-air, then plummet to the rocks below, a year and a half ago.

That and other things.

(Not that Edee had re-entered her relationship with Richard to twist herself pretzel-like into the made-to-order woman of Richard's dreams. No, she told herself, never again. Let the ugly stepsisters do that. She'd pushed her foot into a shoe a full size too small before and was through with all that.)

All of which was, roughly, how Edee'd ended up on a stormy December street wearing a chic but not terribly warm jacket, the arm of the man she loved around her shoulders.

Though it was only early evening, it had already been dark for hours. They were walking past a half-boarded-up convenience store, a house with a snowy upholstered couch on its front porch, a coin wash that had a lopsided Christmas tree perched like some brash, brave weed on its roof.

The movie they were walking back from had been odd. It seemed to have been a teenagers' movie and someone had kept kicking the back of Richard's seat. Richard turned in the flickering half-dark of the movie theatre to say, "Stop kicking the seat." He said it several times.

"Do you want to leave?" Edee said. By then they were being pelted with popcorn, even popcorn kernels, and once, in her peripheral vision, she'd seen a crumpled pop can tumble past. She thought maybe they were in an incident of the sort you read about in the papers, the sort that happened in other, larger, probably American cities, and she couldn't understand the movie anyway. Something bad was happening to the people on the screen. One moment they were fine, then they were screaming and splitting open and hatching things out of their bodies in train stations and at parties.

A young couple to Edee's left had taken on the job of defending them and was telling the ones behind to shut up and stop throwing things and stop kicking the seat, and Edee said why didn't they just leave, but Richard said no, he didn't understand the movie either but he would like to stay and see if, after a while, he would.

Walking into the bitter wind on their way back, Edee thought about how frightened she'd been for a moment or two, and how unfazed Richard had been.

"What total brats," she said. "Heaven help *their* supply teacher. But you didn't let them get to you. You were completely calm and even." Or this is what she tried to say, but her lips were so stiff from cold that instead of "even" she said "evil."

"You were completely calm and evil."

Richard looked at her, startled. "That's funny, you said 'evil.' You said I was calm and evil."

Edee was startled herself, and raised her shoulders and palms to the frosty air. She laughed and chattered her teeth in apology.

Richard withdrew his arm from her shoulder, then almost immediately replaced it. He looked intently at her, pulled her a little closer the second time. "Why are you wearing a flimsy coat like that?" he said, feeling the thinness of the fabric on her shoulder. "You need a warm coat. I want to get you a warm coat."

She laughed up at him through the stinging cold. A coat? It didn't seem like Richard to buy her a coat. A muffin, maybe, a second-hand book, a flowerpot he found on top of a neighbour's trash can, but not something as substantial, as costly, or as frank and unironical as a coat.

But before she had time to look away from Richard's sharply jutting face, or to pull her lips shut to warm her teeth, she found that some tentacle from inside herself had already reached out and latched itself firmly onto this idea. Why, she found herself thinking, this was the absolute right gesture for Richard to make. The very notion of Richard buying her a coat steadied her in some way, calmed her, eased something she hadn't known was logjammed in the very centre of her chest. Richard buying her a coat was not only the exact right thing for him to do, she thought; after all the things that had been said and done, it was the *only* thing for him to do.

"A coat?" she asked, crunching her neck and shoulders tight against the cold. She looked at him while a veil of snow lifted from behind him, swirled around them and spiralled toward the green and gold tree on top of the coin wash. "You'll buy me a coat?"

Richard lifted her gloved hand and, without saying anything, without laughing or joking or deflecting in any way, pressed her balled-up fingers to the rough wool scarf at his throat.

They'd just begun to walk once more when Edee stopped.

"Look," she said, her teeth almost chattering. She pointed to a narrow illuminated storefront across the street from them. "They might have coats. I'm pretty sure they'll have coats."

The sign on the window of the store, painted in gold but hard to see now in the dark, read *Ragtime Vintage Clothes*. The narrow window held a mannequin wearing a red cape that looked as if it had once belonged to the ringmaster of a circus and, beside him, a suspended birdcage, strings of cascading beads, a cane with a brass bird's head handle, a many-headed laughing Buddha.

Edee pushed the door open and amber light sparkled from melting ice crystals as they stamped their feet, shook the snow off their hair. The air was generous with warmth, scented with patchouli, cedar and some not unpleasant musty smell, like that of old books.

The store was like a secret gypsies' cave. Not the dank, dripping affair a gypsies' cave likely was in reality, Edee thought, but the way a gypsies' cave was supposed to be, the way gypsies' caves were in fairy tales. Beaded and sequinned garments were pinned high against one wall, while a yellowed wedding dress and antique lace veil adorned another. A glass closet held rhinestone necklaces, turquoise bracelets, silver watches. Another glass case displayed a tomato-shaped teapot, tin toys, lacquered boxes, antique salt and pepper shakers. The proprietor of the shop, an ancient woman with a dark green Chinese jacket and flowing peach hair, steamed clothes in an alcove to the side.

"Look," Edee said, pointing to a miniature tartan vest and matching bow tie. "My baby had those. Jeremy had a set like that." She looked up at Richard. "My baby who is now twenty and living on the other side of the continent."

Richard leaned down over her shoulder from behind and pressed his cold cheek against her slowly warming one.

He's different, Edee thought, catching a glimpse of their two faces together in the mirror at the back of the jewellery case. He's changed. Once Richard—originally of a more elevated social class and a more conventional mindset than Edee—might have had some double-edged comment to make about a clip-on bow tie, a polyester tartan vest or a son who chose to live thousands of miles away from his mother. But there was something different about Richard now. He seemed less settled around the face, less shined and polished, less shipshape than his previous self. His old handsomeness had been scraped thin.

For the first time it occurred to Edee that Richard had also suffered during their separation. She'd originally hoped he *would* suffer, when he destroyed things between them. She'd openly wished suffering upon him. But Richard had, she decided, a shiny, hard, shellacked exterior that protected him from the world. Wind and cold didn't get to him, neither did sun or rain. Richard was not capable of suffering—or so she had believed. Neither, she told herself, was he capable of love. How else could Richard be explained, she asked herself at the time.

But the face she saw beside her own in the mirror now was not the same face she'd seen a year and a half ago. This face looked exposed, almost raw, broken open.

"We don't have to get a coat," Edee said, turning to him and embracing him, softening like toffee in the amber light. "I just wanted to get warm. Aren't you glad we came in? Isn't this a marvellous store?"

"But I do want to buy you a coat," Richard insisted. "I want to get you a warm one." Saying this, he turned his attention to the rack of women's coats and began separating them one by one, examining each coat with a kind of attention and determination that intrigued her.

•   •   •

By the time they broke up a year and a half ago, Richard was unhappy on a number of fronts.

Edee (he said) had not lifted him up and out of himself. She had not forced him, for example, to go skinny-dipping, or inspired him to write a sonnet.

He complained about a chipped blue coffee table she had not got around to replacing.

He accused her of putting four different kinds of beans into her lasagna. (When she had used only *one*!)

He said she was not bubbly. (Bubbly! She'd forgotten to be bubbly!)

He said she did not cause the air to smoulder when she stepped into the room.

"Smoulder!" shrieked Edee, tugging two handfuls of her own hair. "*Smoulder?* Smoulder *and* effervesce? Which? When?" At this point she was talking to her friend Christine, who was involved in the aftermath.

She'd been too stunned to say much of anything to Richard. She'd left his place on a blood-warm spring evening, walked back to her own apartment, turned off her answering machine, placed an order to get her locks changed, then lay down on the bed without taking off her shoes.

Two weeks later she went to visit her son in Nanaimo. Jeremy seemed not unhappy to see her, but once, when he found her weepy in front of a late night show on television, he threw a wet bath towel hard on the floor. "What goes around comes around," he told her. A reference to her part in the failure of her original marriage, which he had not yet forgiven her.

When she returned home, she set about pulling herself back into shape, in much the same dogged, dispirited way she might go about trying to salvage a sweater that had got into a disastrously wrong cycle of the wash. She prescribed for herself a regimen of exercise. She learned two soups from a book on Thai cooking. She took a course in black-and-white photography. She went for dinners with a retired radio sound technician whom Christine's sister-in-law's friend passed on to her. She worked through a series of audiotapes on how you must become your own best friend.

It felt like treading water somewhere in the middle of the Atlantic. It felt like a life sentence.

One afternoon Edee left the particular school where she was supplying that day, stopped to get her tea leaves read, then went directly home and called Richard.

"Richard. This is Edee. Do you want to go for coffee?" Dippers, vases, cups: all these portents of plenty were in her teacup, but even more than that, she knew. She could feel something like a pencil line of gold around herself. She had no doubt he would be pleased to hear from her.

"Now?" he said. "I mean, now is good, but I was just putting the cat out."

Richard was devoted to his elderly cat, originally his mother's, so Edee, correctly, did not interpret this as a rebuff. She waited through a "row-oow-ooow"—a cat yowl performed for comic effect—shouts of "closing time," the brief clink of glass near the receiver. Finally he was back, somewhat out of breath.

"There. It's out. Where should we go?" The flat, easy, humorous tone of his voice told her they were picking up where they'd left off.

"At least he's not boring," she said defensively to Christine—that jealous sister!—who criticized. When Christine didn't answer, Edee clicked her fingers soundlessly in the air and attempted a wobbly joke, something she'd overheard in a hallway at school. "The man, like, moves *air.*"

"*Talk.* You can't just slide back into things. You have to *talk,*" Christine counselled. But where had talk got *her*? Christine was a single woman, a potter who also taught handicrafts to young offenders and knit wool socks with Nordic designs for her friends at Christmas. It was a meaningful life, disciplined, probably vibrant in its own way. But it was also a difficult life, an almost ascetic life, and Edee did not think she was cut out for it.

.   .   .

"What about this one?" Richard said, holding up an impossibly narrow sheepskin coat.

Richard turned the rack, twisting each coat on its hanger to examine it more closely, and Edee glanced up at him, seeing the muscles of his jaw tighten as he pitted himself against the demands of this task, finding a warm coat for her. With his bony jawline, his intense gaze, his heroic determination, he might have been Lord Nelson at Trafalgar or Wolfe on the Plains of Abraham.

This clearly was not easy for him. He was, by all appearances, pitted against a powerful foe. Who was this adversary? Richard's adversary was, Edee guessed, none other than Richard himself.

Edee'd seen the warring sides of Richard before. She'd seen the Richard who had—with infinite care—built up a fine and intricate structure between them. And she'd seen the Richard who—propelled by nothing she understood—had kicked that same structure down again.

What more worthy adversary, Edee asked herself, than your own baser, darker self?

"Sweet, gallant Richard," Edee murmured, hiding her smile in his sleeve.

"Are you helping?" he asked, with mock or real severity—with Richard it could be hard to tell. His eyes softened, but he asked again, "Why are you looking at teapots? We're supposed to be looking at coats."

"That's the kind of store this is," Edee said. "If you're looking at teapots, you find a coat. And if you're looking at coats, well, there you go—you might find one that way too."

Richard held up an embroidered suede coat with a questioning look, a short fleece-lined imitation leather coat, a navy wool pea jacket.

"Here's one," said Edee, extracting a long coat from a crowded rack nearer the back. "It looks big, though. And, well, awfully . . . *brown*."

She took it to the large three-way mirror near the door, just as a young blond man came in, bringing a gust of icy air with him. Edee pulled on the coat, looked at her reflection a moment, then spun around.

"Don't I look like Anna Karenina in this coat?" she laughed, shy but pleased. The coat came down to her ankles, and the colour, which was closer to taupe than brown, set off her silver hair rather stunningly, or so she thought.

Richard watched, though his face remained tilted downward. Then he came forward and read the price tag dangling from her wrist.

"I don't believe it," he accused. "You tried it on without looking at the price tag first. Didn't you?"

She looked up at him, her smile still on her face like a scrap of paper loose on the floor.

"I was watching you," he continued in apparent disbelief. "You didn't even *glance* at the price first. Aren't you the tiniest bit *curious* about the price before you try something on?"

The light in the mirror gathered into one tight point then dispersed again.

"No!" Edee said as grandly as she could. "I *never* look at the price tag first!" She didn't. If she had the money—and sometimes she did—then money was not her first consideration. She couldn't believe they were debating this.

But because Richard was still looking pale and beleaguered, she shook her head and added, "The kind of stores I go to, I don't *need* to look at the price tag first." Then she lifted the price tag dangling from the taupe coat and read it. It had more figures in it than she expected.

"Oh." She dropped it again.

"You're paying for the *name* with a coat like that," Richard said with an air of vindication. "You're not getting *warmth*. I thought it was *warmth* we were after."

"Here's another coat that's just come in," the proprietor of the store offered. "I've just finished pricing it."

Edee walked back to the middle of the store, took a purple and green coat from the woman's hands. There seemed to be a very high-pitched whistle inside the store, like a sound just outside the range of hearing. She noticed that the young blond man was looking at cufflinks and watches, singing to himself, and hopping oddly from foot to foot. Returning to the mirror, she instinctively gave him plenty of space to himself.

Edee pulled on the purple and green coat and examined herself in the three-way mirror. The coat was a sturdy nylon parka with a hood, Velcroed cuffs, a drawstring waist. It had large patch pockets, no doubt useful for Kleenexes and bus transfers, plastic toggles to adjust the tightness of the hood, a two-way zipper.

There was nothing wrong with a coat like this. People wore coats like this. She'd seen them, at bus stops and at shopping centres. The coat was lined, not at all heavy, very likely machine washable. Certainly it was warmer than the black jacket. Richard wanted to buy her a warm coat. Why not let him buy her this one?

"Look," Richard announced suddenly, "it's not working." He was standing in the shadows behind the coat rack and in front of twinkly evening wear. Edee could see his head behind her in the mirror, but could not make out his features. "It wasn't such a great idea," he said.

Edee turned and looked at him in the shadows. The high-pitched whistle must have something to do with the steamer, she thought.

"Not every idea's going to be a crackerjack idea," Richard said.

"*I* think it's a crackerjack idea," she answered. "This coat seems warm. It seems . . . well . . . it seems *just fine*. I would be delighted if you bought this coat for me."

"*Just fine*," Richard said, pouncing on her words. "*Just fine*. Why settle for a coat that's only *just fine*? A coat should be terrific. A coat should be fantastic. It should lift you up and sweep you out the door. But look at you. You're not happy with it."

"I *am* happy," she said unhappily.

"It's gone flat," Richard accused, gesturing with his thin white palm in the dimness. "The fun has gone out of it."

Edee stared at Richard, who was still in the shadows, stared at the proprietor, who was still steaming clothing, stared at the young blond man, who was talking to himself and dancing now, jigging on one foot then the other. Then she saw another head wearing an odd little elf cap just over the young man's elbow. The young blond man had a child under his coat with him, both of them leaning back easily from the fulcrum of the young man's hips, like branches of a single tree, or heads of the same Buddha. The young man continued to bounce and sing to the baby.

What an enormous thing to have a child, Edee thought. What an enormous thing to connect with anyone, ever. It occurred to her that they were all very small and whirling around in the enormous and infinite blackness. How could they have any context, any *frame*, except in terms of each other?

As Edee watched, the young man bundled up his coat and was gone, banging the door behind him. A moment later the door burst open again, unleashing a blizzard of wind and snow into the store. The proprietor hurried to the door, her peach hair blowing, and Edee caught her own image in the mirror.

She saw a silver-haired woman—a woman no longer young—her wild hair catching the light, all herself of one piece, of one breath, of one name—all of her glorious in her own right. Behind her she could see a dark swirl of wedding gowns, teapots, children's toys, tiaras, handbags, lamps, and Richard's face too—a yellowed bulb of ginger—all of it, everything, blowing away, darkening, receding into distance.

Suddenly the door slammed shut again. The wind vanished. The objects in the room settled into approximations of their earlier places.

"Hello? Hel-*lo*!" Richard called, his manner jocular, his features once again snapped neatly into their proper places. *"All aboooard!"*

Silken banners of snow, yellow, orange and pink with city light, tumbled past the window.

"None of the coats had your name on them," Richard insisted, still in his humorous manner. "None of them had *Edee* written all over them. Did they?" He jostled her elbow in a joking way. "They didn't, now, did they?"

She looked up at him in the mirror. She found herself almost surprised to see him still there, surprised to see him beckoning with raised eyebrows and his old shipshape smile, surprised to see him leaning attentively forward. She turned to face him.

He was holding the black woollen jacket open for her.

myna

Myna is up to ladies' girdles when Lester comes back in. The noise of the pump pours into the room, then muffles a bit when he shuts the door.

Myna chooses the girdles almost at random, flipping the pages of the catalogue as she places her square finger quickly in turn on each one she's picked. With brassieres, she takes longer. The models are lined up sideways and overlapping, like the ribs of a fan, displaying a rainbow of available colours. There are scientific-looking cross-sections of some of the features available—padding, wiring, bone inserts. Some of the brassieres have little trap doors that can be unlatched to feed a baby. Myna stares at these, but when she chooses, she chooses the strapless black from one page, the low-cut lacy apricot from the next.

"Do you ever play the catalogue game?" Myna asks Lester. "What you do is you pick one thing from each page. One item per page, period." She flips to men's shirts and slides the catalogue across the tabletop toward him. "Here, you try it," she says, grinning up at him.

Myna's smile is her best feature; Miss Kay, her typing teacher, had said so when Myna was still in school and still in Miss Kay's typing class. Miss Kay was young and pretty and from England. She hardly ever yelled at the class, though once she'd gone three days without speaking, writing instructions on the blackboard only. Sometimes she stayed after school to talk to the girls and gave them tips on what to do at a dance if you weren't dancing (smile), how to make yourself look thinner (tuck in your pelvis) or what to do when you're smarter than your boyfriend (don't let him know). For example, if your boyfriend got his car stuck in the mud, you should say, "This silly car!" and not blame the boy, even if it was his fault.

Myna was glad to know this. She probably would have got out and pushed. That's what her mother did. She felt lucky to be tipped off.

Miss Kay said Myna had good bone structure and should walk as if she were carrying a basket of cherries.

Myna would rather be small and delicate. Her ears are delicate, though. Buddy had said so. "You got ears like a china doll," he once said.

"Let's not be going overboard," she answered tartly. It seems a shame to her, though, having her good looks wasted on her ears.

Lester shifts in his gumboots inside the door but doesn't move to sit down with the catalogue. The toothpick in the corner of his mouth moves out, in, out again.

"I was thinking," he says above the noise of the pump, then stops. He pushes the peak of his cap back with a finger. His face is red and lined, but his forehead above the line of his cap is pale, blue-veined, almost private-looking. "What I was thinking," he says, one side of his mouth clamped down on the toothpick, "come on to town. Pick what it needs. Shirt. Pants. Hat. Maybe." He looks at her with his pale blue eyes, then quickly down at his boots. He rubs his hand over his mouth and chin.

Myna stares hard at the calendar on the wall beside Lester's shoulder. She is thinking about how Lester noticed without seeming to notice, and about whether that makes him sneaky or polite.

Finally she stands up. She guesses it's not exactly a secret now. She planned never to set foot in town again, but on the other hand, why shouldn't she set foot there? Doesn't she have as much right to go into town as anybody else? She feels settled, as if she has folded something and put it in a drawer. For the time being, at least.

"Diapers," Myna says, steadying herself on the edge of the table. "It needs diapers, pins and some of those little matching outfits at the Bay. This baby is not going to be dressed in anywhich thing. This baby is going to always be dressed in everything-matching."

The pump shuts off. The silence in the room is sudden and heavy, and there is a faint smell of kerosene.

"Wee-el!" Lester says. He wipes his mouth on the top of his hand and grins. His toothpick bristles up like an exclamation mark.

Myna changes to her best. She's glad now that her mother threw her best dress out onto the road—along with all her other clothes—that night she figured out about the baby. The dress is not homemade. Myna bought it herself at the Bay with the money she'd saved from waitressing. It has a blue velvet top with rhinestone buttons and a flowery satin circle skirt. The large blue flowers on the skirt are flecked, as if with dew, by glittery blue sequins. The dress is good enough to wear anywhere, although up to now Myna has saved it for Saturdays when the older girls, like herself, dress up and walk arm in arm downtown past the Co-op and the Red and White, the barber shop and the beer parlour, then past the Elite Café, looping back down on the other side of the street past the poolroom, Marvin Motors, the Bay and the Roxy Theatre.

Myna can get the dress over her head now, but the zipper at the side won't do up. Then she remembers the stole. It will cover the zipper. It's June, but it's early and the mornings are still cold. Why not go in a real lady?

Buddy gave her the stole, a fur, he called it. White fox, he said, and it was, in fact, slightly yellowish, the way a winter rabbit can look running across a field.

Myna had worn it to school with a straight purple skirt,

seamless nylons, black spikes, her stomach sucked in and her hair bobby-pinned into a French roll. The grade twelve girls in the washroom had said it was a fake, but they were jealous. Buddy was really cute with wavy black hair combed back into a ducktail. He didn't dress like the high school boys, with their plaid shirts and blue jeans or work pants. Buddy wore dress pants and dress shirts with his sleeves rolled up to the elbow, like the other businessmen in town. He was through with school, ran the Rosaline Rooms, and drove his own car, a two-tone yellow and black Pontiac.

Lucky for the stole, Myna thinks, and twirls around as best she can, watching the skirt circle and glint blue sparks around her.

Lester has the horses harnessed by the time she gets out, with an extra blanket on the seat. The seat is so high and the ladder so steep, he has to help hoist Myna up.

"Don't go getting a heart attack," Myna says, settling herself.

Lester climbs up beside her and takes the reins. The horses strain and brace themselves because the water is heavy and they have to go slightly downhill to get to the road. The dripping wagon creaks and lurches, and Myna grabs the rail in front of them once or twice because it feels for a moment as if they might tip. Pretty soon they are down on the highway, which is bumpy with gravel but level.

Myna checks her hair with her hands, straightens the stole and arranges her skirt around herself, puffing it up so it glints and sparks in the sun and you can't even tell about the baby.

The air smells fresh and leafy, and the road is lined with green weeds and yellow dandelions. Birds are clothespinned along the telephone wire and call out noisily to one another. Not too far off, a woodpecker is hammering away. Myna thinks it was a good idea to come. Lester's place in the bush is fine, especially the front room with the big red Chinese lantern, but how long can you play cards and listen to the radio? She's been at Lester's for a little over a month now.

•   •   •

This is the same road Myna had been on that first night she came to Lester's, but it was much colder then and almost dark. She had been going to the highway to wait for the bus. It was muddy, and although she tried to walk mostly in the packed-down tracks in the centre of the road, mud still oozed over the tops of her shoes. Whenever she heard a car or truck approaching, she moved over but kept walking. She didn't want to talk to anyone. Then another car whipped past, not bothering to slow down at all, splattering her with mud. Her clothes, her arms, her legs, even her face and hair, were spattered with tiny gobs of mud. That's when she shrieked at the red tail lights and sat down on her cardboard box at the side of the muddy road, her nose and fingers freezing, her feet cold and sore from the mud.

She was crying because of the mud. Not because her

mother had screamed, "No better than an Indian!" and had thrown her clothes onto the road, ruining Myna's powder-blue Ban-Lon pullover and matching cardigan. Not because her brothers sat silently over their supper of pork sausages, mashed potatoes and sauerkraut, one of them with his hand clamped over his eyes, crying, and the other one not crying at all. Not because her father stood on the front steps moving his lips soundlessly before he finally said, "You make your bed and now you got to lie on it," and gave her twenty-seven dollars or thereabouts, two tens, a five and some change. Myna had been thrown out before, but never with her clothes and twenty-seven dollars.

As she sat, crying into her hands, on her box in the mud, she thought she heard the creaking and banging of a wagon and a team of horses coming down the road behind her.

She immediately stopped crying, sat up straight and waited for them to pass. But she heard the horses stop slightly behind her, jingle their harness, snort their surprise. Finally they pulled up alongside her.

Myna didn't even need to look around, although she did. There was only one person, besides the milkman, who dragged around town with a team of horses.

"Go away, Lester Mulhoon!" she yelled, lifting one arm to wipe her nose on her sleeve. "Get out of here and leave me alone!"

Lester Mulhoon, the water man, lived in a tarpaper shack behind the Stampede Grounds. Buddy, who had gone there once to get a tow for his car, claimed Lester lived right in the same shack as his horses.

"I jest not," Buddy said to the men drinking coffee in the café. Buddy held up his hand as if taking an oath. "The self-same shack. You heard it here, from none other than yours truly." Buddy's mother and sister were schoolteachers, and some of their schoolteachery way of talking had rubbed off on Buddy.

Lester sat on the seat of his water wagon without saying anything. Lester hardly ever said anything. Lester's father, Old Man Mulhoon, who used to drive the water wagon until Lester took over, had been the same.

After a few minutes Lester cleared his throat, as if waiting to be paid for a barrel of water. Finally he said, "Hey there," a kind of question.

"Straw's cheaper, grass is free," Myna snapped back, folding her arms for warmth and looking straight ahead. She was wearing her muddy powder-blue sweater, which possibly she could get clean with a bar of Sunlight soap if she got a chance to do it soon enough.

"Want a ride?" he said.

After a moment Myna answered him. "Oh, why not." Then she climbed up, hanging on to her ruined and muddy box. "I'm going to the highway to take the bus," she said over the sound of the wagon, which had begun to move again. The twenty-seven dollars was more than enough to get to Grande Prairie, where she planned to buy new nylons and a wedding ring, then get a waitressing job. The bus would pass along the highway shortly after one a.m.

The water wagon creaked as they bumped and splashed along the road. Everything on the ground was getting dark now, the road, the trees, the horses and themselves, but the sky still held the light, and a skinny moon was coming up straight ahead.

Lester didn't look at Myna, or talk to her, or bother her at all, and Myna liked that. She liked moving along in the dark like that, under a still-shining sky.

"My husband passed away," Myna said, as much to herself as to Lester. She was surprised how easy she found it, practising the story she'd worked out for herself here in the dark. Although Lester remained silent and kept on facing straight ahead, she slipped her ringless, mud-splattered left hand under the box on her knee. "Hunting accident," she added, glancing sideways at him. "The gun went off with no warning whatsoever."

Spoken out loud like that, her story sounded much finer and sadder than she expected. Especially as she thought of herself going out to wait for the bus on the night road, alone now, and with a baby on the way. She touched the side of her cheek with the heel of her hand, then reached up to smooth her hair.

Soon she saw the dark shapes of the stands at the Stampede Grounds come up on the left and she knew they were getting close to Lester's place, which was back off the highway where she would wait for the bus. The moon was shining a steady pale yellow and the sky was the colour of the ink they had to use at school, blue-black. They were not allowed to use Mediterranean Blue, Sea Green or Red, even though these colours were prettier and the drugstore sold them for the same price.

"If you would kindly get me a flashlight," Myna instructed Lester, for she would need a flashlight to signal the bus.

"Bus isn't for a while," Lester said, and stopped. Then, after she thought that was all he meant to say, she heard him clear his throat and add, "You could wash up."

"Listen to the pot calling the kettle black!" Myna said. Feature that, she thought. Lester Mulhoon, who slept with his horses, telling *her* to wash up!

The wagon lurched as they seemed to go up a level, and Myna hung on. The road was so dark and so far down and she was having a good time up here on the wagon. She made no protest as the wagon cut off the main road and onto the side road that led to Lester's shack farther back in the bush.

•   •   •

That was the end of April and now's it's June, school's almost out. Myna guesses she's failed grade eleven, which is not what she'd planned. She'd planned to finish grade eleven and go on to study at Marvel Beauty School in the city. She hopes she never has to see the report card saying *Failed*, or possibly even *Expelled*. Three boys got expelled last year for skipping math to play pool, so she supposes she could be expelled for doing what she's done.

The horses are pulling hard but steady, and early as it is, Myna hears a truck come up behind them, then pass. It's a green Fargo pickup, Elmo Stenson and Elmo Junior. The truck slows right in front of them while the Elmo Stensons talk, stare, grin. Then they spin their tires, shooting gravel out behind them, leaving the water wagon in a storm of dust.

The horses try to veer into the ditch.

"Bloody sons of bitches, stupid blockheads," Lester says, but in a soothing way for the horses, which he holds to the road.

Before long they're passing the dog catcher's shack under the bridge, the dairy, then they're into town.

With each stop, Lester has to get off, undo the hose, drag it to the barrel, while Myna waits on the wagon. Sometimes people come out with a pail or a pot they want filled. Some people pay Lester on the spot, others owe him. Lester wears a pencil above his ear but doesn't write anything down.

"Lester," Myna calls out, "is the H_2O always such a big hit?" She sees Mrs. Creamore holding back her kitchen curtains to watch, and Old Lady Kopko squinting at them from behind her front gate. Myna doesn't mind people getting an eyeful. She's high up on the wagon and she's wearing her best.

The stole is too warm now and Myna has to drape it off one shoulder, taking care to cover the side where the zipper won't do up. She strokes the stole with her free hand. It is hot and silky, like a dog in the sun.

Next they pass the baseball diamond beside the school. There's the flagpole where Edmund Cox froze his tongue in grade four, there's the parking lot where the older boys fought at noon hour, rolling furiously in the dirt then shaking hands in the end.

Why, Lester was one of those boys, she remembers in surprise. When she'd just started school and was coming back after lunch, she would stop and watch the older boys fight, a privilege the bus kids did not have. She remembers seeing Lester, red-faced and old-looking even then, pale spiky hair, rolling in the dirt, his arms punching like pistons.

"I remember you," she says. "You ripped Arthur Boyle's shirt. And his lip was bleeding. The Boyles were important. You must of got the strap."

"No. I dunno," says Lester, rubbing his face as if tired. "It couldn't a been me."

Usually boys were proud of the lickings they'd taken in school. Myna had never seen anyone not at least get a good story out of it.

The deliveries beyond the school take longer than Myna expected and she wishes they had a radio up here. Then they cut across a few streets and suddenly are on her street, near her house, the house where she's lived for her whole life, except for the last month.

It seems to her the horses slow to almost a stop in front of her house, although her mother has a well of her own and never buys water. Sometimes her mother lets the neighbours use her well and other times she cuts them off, if they've done something wrong, like stepping on her flowers or spitting in the yard.

Myna looks at the little house with its brown, brick-patterned siding, its wire fence and the flowers in their military rows between—dahlias, not yet blooming, marigolds, asters, baby's breath, irises, and bleeding heart on the side. There is a wash freshly hung on the line, and rags spread on the side bushes to dry and bleach in the sun, but no movement anywhere.

As they move past the house, Myna sees her bedroom window at the side. Her white bed is in there, and she thinks she can see just a bit of the padded vinyl headboard. The bed is a double, so large it takes up almost the whole room. She'd wanted twin beds, like another girl she knew, but her mother said no, double is better, she could take it with her when she got married. Her mother was saving family allowances, too, so that when Myna married she could buy a chesterfield and matching chair.

Why should she care about her mother planning and saving all those years? I didn't ask her to do that, did I, Myna tells herself. Who asked her to do that, anyway?

The water wagon crosses the main street by the clinic, and Lester delivers to the Elite Café where Myna used to waitress. Although you were allowed to eat whatever you wanted

when you were waitressing—except for the T-bone steaks—
Myna hated waitressing. People always wanted something:
tea, even when the coffee was closer, raisin pie as an after-
thought to their coffee, ice cream with their Jell-O. They
complained if the crackers came after the soup, if their ham-
burger arrived *with* a slice of onion or *without* a pickle. It was
Myna's view that they should eat what they were given.

When they pull away from the Elite, Myna suddenly realizes where Lester's going next.

"I'm getting off," she says, lurching to her feet and almost
over the rail in front of them.

Lester catches her by the arm and steadies her, but by
then the horses have pulled up outside the Rosaline Rooms.

The Rosaline Rooms are a wooden, two-storey building
painted blue. There is long grass in the front, and the smell
of cats. The grass and the road in front are littered with rocks,
broken glass, cigarette butts, even the skull of a cow that has
been in the weeds beside the steps as long as Myna can
remember. The sun catches on a few bottles that have been
left in a line at the side of the road, and the glare hurts
Myna's eyes.

Lester doesn't pull off to the side like Myna is one hundred percent sure she's seen him do before, but stops right
out in front and is already dragging a hose off to the side.

Well, this is a fine state of affairs, Myna tells herself. And
me stuck up on top like a clipped chicken. She stares severely
straight ahead for a time, taking care to hang on to the stole

on her shoulder. Lester is taking forever to fill the barrels at the side. Still, no one inside the Rosaline Rooms seems to be paying attention.

Maybe no one *will* pay attention, she tells herself. After all, it's only the water wagon, and who ever pays attention to the water wagon?

After a time it seems safe to look inside, and Myna can pick out the men sitting and smoking in the dark lobby. That's Pete Symington with the cowboy hat. There's Bit Player the barber, little, almost bald and with no hat. There's Alvin Shanks with the grease monkey cap he always wears, even in the rooms upstairs. She knows they are smoking, not saying much, tapping their cigarettes into the monkey ashtray or dropping them on the oiled wood floor.

She doesn't see Buddy, but he could be there. Buddy could be sitting on the stool behind the counter right now. She would like to see Buddy, except for knowing that Buddy doesn't want to see her. She'd put things so poorly. "Take your time, Myna," Miss Kay used to say when they did their practice job interviews in front of the class. "Think first. Think before you speak." But she'd forgotten that advice when she needed it the most.

What she'd said—and not in the friendliest way—was, "I'm in trouble, Buddy! And *you're* the one to blame!" That was when he hit her.

Buddy had started to change before that, though. He'd started not being there when she delivered sandwiches from the Elite. He never invited her to their upstairs parties anymore, where they smoked, played cards, and drank whisky and Coke from paper cups.

She's glad she never gave the stole back, though, even though he said she had to, that it was his sister's.

"What a sad tale to tell," she'd said when he asked. She dropped the three hot western, two ham and three turkey sandwiches on the counter in the lobby. "Too bad. It's mine now."

She'd started throwing up in the mornings and knew she was in trouble. Either that or she had cancer. If she gave the stole back, everything was over. Her mother had had such a crazy fit about it in the first place, how could she give it back now?

Someone inside says something and the men cough and laugh a little. Someone spits. Probably Alvin.

"Got the time to step in, Myna?" someone says, low and gravelly, but she hears it.

A wave of hotness passes over her, leaving her dizzy. Suddenly her dress feels all wrong. It's too small and is pulling across the chest, and the sequins look like cheap, ordinary things, not like dew at all. Sweat trickles down her side under the stole. She wants to jump off the wagon and run.

Buddy is there, standing in the doorway. His furry arm is in the bright sun, but the rest of him is scissored off by the shade of the doorway. It is so bright she can hardly look up, but when she does, he is just staring, no movement in his face or in his eyes. He is staring like a stranger through a bus window.

"The fur," he says, really quiet, without moving. "Take it off. Take it off and throw it down."

Lester is rolling up the hose and in sixty seconds they'll be gone. Fifty seconds. Forty seconds.

Where *is* Lester? Everything looks dark around the edges. It seems to her that Lester is moving very slowly, like a picture on a movie screen when the projector jams.

Lester is ambling slowly back toward the Rosaline Rooms. Myna can't believe it. What is he doing? Lester doesn't collect until the end of the month.

Myna watches while Lester positions himself sideways in the littered yard. He lifts off his cap, rakes down his pale hair with his fingers, replaces his cap.

The men inside continue to sit. Buddy still stands in the doorway, his feet apart, arms crossed. No one moves. Then Buddy begins to rock, very slowly, from his heels to the balls of his feet and back again.

Lester squats, scoops a handful of stones from the ground, shakes them between his hands like dice. It is very quiet and bright.

Lester stands and—quickly now—throws a stone at the line of bottles standing on the edge of the road. He hits a Pepsi bottle, hits a beer bottle, breaking off the top, then hits a green ginger ale bottle. He throws again and hits the largest one, the Five Star whisky bottle. The Five Star whisky bottle shatters loudly, one of the horses rears and paws the air, and the broken glass scatters across the road like ice.

Lester walks back to the wagon, climbs on. He settles with his elbows on his spread knees, picks up the reins, and the horses pull easily away, their load lighter.

At the corner, the horses, knowing their route by heart, turn left without a pause, heading for the Bay. Leaning with the turn, Myna looks back along the straight grey road. The Rosaline Rooms are far back now, a duller, flatter blue than the sky above, which is bright and very high.

There is someone standing in the dark doorway, but it is hard to tell for sure who it is, because the horses are moving quickly and the road is rough. A fresh breeze catches them rounding the corner and, looking back, Myna sees the water trickling from the wagon, flying back in threads of silver.

viewfinder

The frog stuck out his long pink tongue—*thwap! thwap!*—two flies in one swallow! *Thwap-thwap-thwap!* Three in one blow!

"Miles?"

That was his mother. As usual. (Why did his mother always *want* something?) The frog on the screen held up a card. *Your score is 41.*

All *right*! He hit Play Again.

"Miles?" His mother was at his elbow this time, half befuddled but relentlessly bossy, bringing with her a new floral scent underlaid by the increasingly familiar chemical smell of hair dye. Without changing the position of his arms or head, without lifting his hand from the mouse, Miles looked down, observing her flat brown shoes, her nyloned ankles, the odd habit she had of rising slightly to her toes as she spoke. "Miles?"

He rolled back his chair and bent to scoop up Cleo, his cat, who huddled underneath his desk. But Cleo kicked suddenly and hard, shooting under the bed and away from him. Miles shook his hand and sucked furiously at the web between his thumb and his forefinger.

"See?" he accused, looking up at his mother. "She doesn't like it here."

"Come out and watch TV with him, Miles. Remember? I told you I needed you to watch TV with him."

His mother, Gail, had a generic mother's face, the slightest bit withered, like a week-old balloon, but lately her hair had taken on a life of its own. It gleamed like a black football helmet around her face, solid and unmoving, impressive in its own right, like a microwave tower or a ship in full sail. Her clothes were all flappy and silky now, and she wore jangly necklaces and large, irregularly shaped metallic earrings that looked like they'd been salvaged by a wrecker. This was the way she'd taken to dressing now that Miles's father, Terence, had had a stroke and she'd got a job—her first "real" job in Miles's memory—as supply librarian in the public library system.

"Your hair looks weird," Miles offered, his voice without inflection. He was flat on his bed now, wincing as he nursed his injured hand.

"The box said *Mahogany*," she said, touching it cautiously, as if it were an abandoned parcel in the subway. "Better dark than light, though. It fades so fast when I wash it."

"Yeah. Well. You got your basic roadkill look down to a T."

"Oh dear," she said, but in the tone of one accustomed to battling off bad news. She stepped to his closet door and stood frontwards then sideways to check herself in his mirror. She rotated one shoulder then the other, tilted her head and watched the light glint off her hair. "It doesn't look *that* bad. Does it? In fact, I think it looks *good*." She looked over her shoulder at him. "Doesn't it?"

"Forget it. You have no sense of humour. Why did the chicken cross the road?" Miles leapt out of bed and grinned down at her, bouncing on his bare feet, jostling her with his elbow. He was taller than her by half a foot, even in his baggy camouflage pants only half as wide. "Why did the chicken cross the road, Mom?" he asked again, bouncing along beside her to the kitchen.

"Don't keep me in suspense, Miles. Oh, shoot! Did I give him his six o'clock pills?" She dumped the bottle of tiny blue pills onto the counter, took off her glasses, then bent close to count them.

"To get away from fowl language!" Miles bent down to see her face as she scooped the pills back into their bottle and snapped on the lid. "Get it? *Fowl language?*" He clutched the top of the fridge in a show of laughter, then followed her to the bathroom.

"No, listen!" he said. "This one's better! Why did the chicken cross the road? To get to the hospital! The farmer had a stroke!" And he dangled from the shower-curtain rod to laugh again.

"Don't put your full weight on that, hon, it's going to come right off the wall."

When his mother was called in for a full day at the library, she hired a woman from the agency, but when she was called in for the shorter evening shift, Miles had to babysit his dad.

Miles watched his mother in the bathroom mirror as she took off her glasses, began to swab blue gunk onto her eyelids.

He tiptoed close to her. "Boo! You jiggled!" Then he gave his maniacal laugh. "Did you hear that, Mom? *Yah-ha-ha-ha-ha!* That's my maniacal laugh."

His mother put her mascara-speckled glasses back on, took Miles's hand and led him to the living room, where his father sat. His father was dressed in a grey jogging suit, had pale bare ankles and white hair spiking up wildly in a rooster's comb.

Gail flipped through the TV guide, ran her finger down one column.

"You going somewhere?" Terence asked, half shouting, his voice indignant, aggrieved, his hands open boxes on his lap.

"'*Wood ducks,*'" Gail read aloud. "'*Visit the wood ducks in their natural habitat. These distinctive perching ducks are denizens of the open woodlands on both sides of Canada and the southeastern U.S.*' Oh. Good, wood ducks are perfect. He likes nature shows, Miles. They're slow and quiet and he seems to follow right along."

"You leaving me alone again?" Terence demanded.

Gail quickly smoothed his hair. "You liked the lemmings, didn't you?" she asked, speaking loudly, for his hearing, never perfect, had slipped along with everything else.

He stared back at her.

"The lemmings, remember? You liked them, Terence." She waited a moment. "The Norwegian lemmings. *On TV*, Terence."

Terence slowly raised his hand and clamped onto her forearm. His eyes had the colour and depth of amber, but he had good days and bad days. Some days he asked Miles how school was, or said if Gail bought a new plug, he and Miles would rewire the living-room lamp. But other days he thought he was still in the hospital and begged to go home. Twice at supper he'd referred to Miles as "that boy," though Gail blamed it on Terence's English childhood, where she was pretty sure a girl or a boy could routinely be called "that girl" or "that boy."

The doctor in the hospital had called Miles and his mother into an office, and on a pad of paper sketched a floppy circle to indicate a brain.

"Most strokes occur this way," the baby-faced doctor explained, darkening a spot like a drop of blueberry jam on the circle. "In a case like this, the prognosis might be more positive, as there might be only one function affected—hearing, speech, your left eyelid if you're lucky." He looked up at them eagerly, inviting them to appreciate the scientific marvel this presented. "The brain is smart. It can relearn," he continued. "But in your husband's—and your father's—case," and here he looked more uneasily at Gail, then at Miles, "his brain scan would look more like this."

He sketched a second circle and, while Miles and his mother watched, jabbed the circle rapidly with the tip of his ballpoint pen, again and again and again, until the circle was shadowed everywhere by tiny, sometimes overlapping, dots.

"In his case," the doctor said, "the strokes are small, but continuous. They have been, in fact, already occurring for some time. We will see his deterioration continue, and the effects of his disabilities rapidly become more pronounced."

Miles felt his mother's shoulder heaving silently against his own, and he was so startled by this, by the diagram and by the ordinariness of the office that had provided no preparation for what was to transpire, that he found himself crying too.

They should post warnings on a room like this, Miles thought. They should post signs that say, *Hello! Brain-Mangled City Ahead!* Or, *Try this on for size: Your Father is Stupid!*

The speckled circle, the one the doctor had drawn to illustrate his father's brain, reminded him of nothing so much as the tomato-shaped pincushion they had in the mending basket at home.

Your Dad: The Pincushion-Brain.

Wiping her face with the heel of her hand, refusing the box of Kleenex the young doctor offered, Gail asked questions, gesturing with both hands, as if arguing their case in a court of law. "Wouldn't it be the other way around? Wouldn't the small strokes be better than the big ones? Wouldn't the pin-sized strokes be more positive?"

The pink-cheeked doctor developed matching pink splotches on his neck, and finally left them in the office with the two brain sketches to compose themselves.

"Where do you think you're going?" Terence asked, his hand clamped on Gail's arm.

"I'm going to work. I have to earn money, Terence. I'm going to work in the library." She removed his hand from her arm and offered him her plasticized library identification card.

Terence held the card between two fingers like a wafer.

"I'm a librarian now, remember?" she said, indicating her card. "But Miles will stay with you, won't you, Miles?" She looked at Miles. *"Won't you, Miles?"*

"Okay, *okay*," Miles answered, dropping backwards onto the couch and jostling his father. "You don't have to keep *telling* me."

"You'll have to go with him when he pees, Miles," his mother added, clipping the identification card to the chain around her neck. She pulled a plastic bag from the hall closet, pulled out a shiny beige handbag, ripped off the price tag and emptied her coat pockets into the handbag. "Did you hear me, Miles? Go with him when he pees. He knows where everything is, but he likes someone to go with him. He gets worried on his own."

"Who *in blazes* is staying with me?" Terence yelled.

"Miles is staying with you, Terence," Gail called over her shoulder. She was pulling on her raincoat, lifting her wrist to the hall light to check her watch. "He'll settle down once I'm gone, Miles. Talk to him. *Talk* to him, Miles, so he realizes."

"The square on the hypotenuse," Miles droned in a flat, mechanical way, "is equal to the sum of the squares on the other two sides."

He waited for her to shut the apartment door, to shake the knob from the outside, to proceed up the four marble steps to the main level. He listened for the muffled thud of the thick glass outside door, watched for the unseemly, overeager flicker of her bulky silhouette as she hurried to the bus stop. (Look at her! He'd never seen her happier! She couldn't wait to leave them!) Then he waited for the commotion she'd generated in the airwaves to subside.

Cleo, now on top of the television set, stared out the window at the shapes of people and umbrellas passing, their dark humped forms bent into the grey wind.

Miles found that, if he squinted through his eyelashes, the silhouettes of passersby outside looked not like passersby at all, but like clouds or shadows billowing past the window. With his eyes squinted like that, the apartment began to feel not at all like a dim basement apartment, but like a high, airy place, a wonderful place, a hotel in some faraway country maybe, with the windows open and the clouds scudding past. Even the air seemed fresher. Wonderful things, adventurous things, could happen, any moment now. But then, when he opened his eyes, they thudded back to the ground with a sickening lurch, back to this dim, shadowy apartment.

Cleo's ears pressed back as the shadows passed, rose slightly when the window cleared, then pressed back again as the next shape bobbled past.

"You're not going to leave me *alone*, are you, Miles?" his father asked, drawing out *alone* like a lonely hound. "You won't leave me *alooooone*?"

"*A* equals pi *R* squared," Miles answered. "Pi equals approximately 3.14159." Somewhere behind his eyes he saw the flash of his brilliance, his wit, then caught the edge of something else, something dark, both red and black, like shame.

But his dad smiled at him with his amber eyes, patted Miles's hand, smiled again. For a moment Terence's eyelids drooped, but he roused himself, looked over immediately to check on Miles, then, reassured, smiled and patted Miles's hand again.

•   •   •

Yesterday, they'd moved from their fourth-floor apartment to this one, exactly below. Their apartment building was not without what Miles's mother annoyingly called "charm"—

marble floors in the entranceway, dark oak curving up the staircase, an occasional leaded window—but it did not have elevators.

Living on what his mother euphemistically called the "ground floor" (it was, in actual fact, four steps *below* the main floor) would, Gail frequently explained, make it considerably easier to take his father out to a waiting cab for medical appointments. She wouldn't have to time it so Miles was home from school to help. She could take Terence out for little walks as he improved, and she indeed foresaw the time they could, all three, take walks together.

This apartment had the exact same floor plan as the last one, and Miles's mother had asked the movers to place everything exactly as it had been arranged upstairs, the couch along one side of the living room, the television set opposite, lamps, coffee tables and armchairs flush against the wall now, to make things easier for Terence. The dining table and chairs were placed along the wall adjacent to the kitchen. Even the framed prints of loons and chickadees were hung over the couch, exactly as they had been upstairs.

"It'll make it easy for your dad," his mother said. "He won't have to learn where the toilet is or where the bedroom is all over again. Everything will be just the same as it was before." She ran over the advantages a few more times, pleased to have come up with this ingenious solution.

Miles wouldn't talk about it anymore. He'd campaigned to move to a nicer, newer building altogether, a place with a pool, a sauna and a weights room. His friend Jack lived in such a building, in the penthouse. How could he ever bring Jack to this place, with his father yelling, "Don't leave me *alooooone!*" and his mother talking too much and too fast and repeating herself constantly, like a CD player jammed on fast-forward.

Not to mention the slush-splattered windows.

Yesterday's move was accomplished in less than a day, and when Miles came home from school, without thinking, he'd gone up to their fourth-floor apartment, now empty and echoey and shocking to behold. There were reverse shadows on the walls, where the furniture and pictures had been, like pictures he'd seen of Hiroshima, where people and objects had been vaporized by the atomic blast, leaving nothing but their silhouettes behind.

He found Cleo curled up in a hot, furry bundle, her heart pounding, in an empty cupboard under the sink. What would have happened to her if he hadn't gone up?

The ground floor (or, more precisely, four steps *below* ground floor) was different. It was lower down, for one thing, leaving more air, more suspended brick and board, to press down on his head and shoulders. There was more street noise, and it was darker, the light now blocked by the apartment building across the street. Now, instead of intersecting wires, asphalt roofs, an occasional patch of city sky, they looked out through splattered windows at bellies and buttocks of rushing people and, beyond that, the blur of traffic. Even as

Miles watched, a leashed Rottweiler approached the building, sniffed the short iron fence that enclosed the lower portion of the window, seemed to try to peer inside, then lifted his leg and urinated on the winter-killed grass.

Cleo stared at all of it, transfixed, her mouth slightly open, like an asthmatic's.

•   •   •

Miles reached for the remote, and a quick succession of fluorescent colours, movement, noise, burst from the television screen. He flicked ahead to *The Price is Right*, then further ahead to what appeared to be live footage of a handcuffed man being led away by police officers, then grainy clips of a video camera's record of a bank robbery.

"A bank robbery! Cool, eh, Dad? Look, they're identifying him by the stitching on his blue jeans!" Miles pointed to the screen, where the video clip was being replayed. "Is the Detroit news cool or what, Dad?"

There was the image of a man, a victim of a shooting, his blood lurid on the screen, an item about a fire, with shots both of the fire, which was spectacular, and of the blackened, steaming aftermath.

Miles thought again of the problem of Jack seeing where he lived. With his regular friend, Mike, whom he'd known since Sunday school days, it wouldn't be so bad, but what if Mike told Jack? Jack with his eyebrow jewellery and his albino rat named Vitriol that he carried in the hood of his baggy black sweatshirt.

"Who's out there? Someone's out there!" Terence yelled, shifting to the edge of the couch and pointing with his entire arm. "What're they after? What do they want?"

Miles shook his head and grinned. You could sell tickets to this place. You really could. "It's nothing, Dad. Don't sweat it. They're just walking by."

"Walking by?" His father was incredulous. He stared again at the movement outside the window. "What do you mean, walking by?"

Miles eased part of the grin off his face to answer. "It's a long story, Dad. You see, Dad, we moved."

Miles could see from his father's face that he found this unbelievable, and Miles could see his point. It *was* somewhat unbelievable, even to himself, sitting here on their own couch, watching their own television, while figures bobbed past the window like puppets on strings.

Jack had bumper stickers all over his bedroom ceiling. Miles's favourite one said *Gravity Sucks*. That pretty much summed things up in Miles's opinion.

Gravity Sucks.

"We moved yesterday, Dad. From the fourth floor to the first floor. You were here. You forgot, that's all. It's okay, don't worry about it, Dad. No sweat, Dad." He tried to give his dad a clumsy high-five. "Relax. Watch TV, Dad."

But his father, agitated now, had already struggled to his feet. "I got to pee," he said through the noise of the television. His voice was argumentative again. "I got to pee."

"Come on, Dad. Sit down. You *don't* have to pee. It's all *right*."

But Terence had already set off, shuffling in his peculiar forward-backward two-step that was in an eventual collision course with the table and chairs.

Finally, Miles got up to deflect his course, to steer him in the direction of the bathroom. Now that his father was in motion, he knew the simplest thing was to get this over with.

The leather soles of his father's slippers scratched and rustled, the sound of a hamster lost inside the couch. Each step advanced another inch toward the bathroom. Two inches forward, one inch back.

Two inches forward, one inch back.

Scratch, scratch, rustle, rustle.

"Hurry," Miles urged, remembering now a worse possibility, that his father might wet himself. He could only guess at the amount of work and commotion that would involve. But his father continued on in the same gear, incredibly slow but steady, his body bent, his head erect, like the prow of an ancient ship.

Finally, in the bathroom, there was the endless positioning and repositioning at the toilet, the questions about whether the lid was up, whether he was in the right place, whether he could go now. He seemed to have some memory in this department at least, Miles noted, for once his father had peed into a bag of groceries, an understandable mistake, his mother'd argued, the top of the brown bag so round and high and not totally unlike the rim of the toilet.

One drop.

A second drop.

Then the part that Miles dreaded, the fruity stench of it. How could such a minute dribble of pee smell so bad? Miles tried not to breathe, braced his forehead against the cool wall to steady himself.

A few more drops.

Miles turned toward the ringing of the phone, but stopped himself. The phone was in the living room.

But then he thought of Jack, and ran for it anyway.

What if his dad started hollering something? Miles turned his back to the bathroom, cupped his hand over the mouthpiece, hunched his shoulders, flipped up the volume on the television.

"Gotcha," he said. A casual tone.

"Hi! How's everything? That doesn't sound like the wood ducks." It was his mother's voice.

Miles's voice was flat. "It's a commercial."

"There's a man here researching how to build himself a bunker in the hills—one of those survivalist types, I guess. He doesn't believe in memberships, so I told him he can't take any books out, he has to do his studying in the library.

And you know the little Chinese girl I told you about? She's here with her grandfather, and—"

"I can't be running to the phone every minute," Miles interrupted, then hung up the receiver.

"Where is everyone? Where the dickens *is* everyone?" Terence was shouting by the time Miles got back to the bathroom.

Taking only shallow breaths, Miles flushed the toilet. His father backed up, an ancient vehicle in reverse, then began the first of his shuffles back to the living room.

The effort of moving so slowly made Miles's scalp hot and itchy. He shut his eyes, guiding himself like a blind man along the cool, smooth wall. When he opened his eyes, they were in the entrance to the living room. His father had stopped walking and was looking up at him, his mouth looped up into a crazy grin.

"I had a stroke, son. And it wasn't a stroke of luck, either." His smile pooled toward one side of his mouth, but both of his eyes shone with humour, with the pleasure of connecting.

Miles stared at him.

His old man was making a joke. He was. And it wasn't a bad joke, either.

He ignored the phone, which began to ring again. He knew it was only his mother and he didn't want to talk to her.

"Why don't they leave us alone?" his father asked, shaking his head against the ringing, lifting a fist toward the shadows passing in the window. "What do they want with us? Why are they here? What're they after?"

Silent laughter bubbled up into Miles's lungs and erupted through his mouth and nose. He clamped his hand across his face, but his laughter only boiled up more forcefully. He rocked backwards and forwards, both hands over his mouth now, his shoulders shaking. This was incredible! This was hilarious! Everything was hilarious! The bodies flickering past the windows were hilarious, his father's puny shaking fist was hilarious, the unanswered phone was funny as hell! The table, the chairs, the chickadees and loons, the actual *floorboards*, were not to be believed!

"What the devil are they after?" Terence demanded, the phone still ringing, the television blaring, the dark shadows still swimming past. "Are they stealing? What do they want? Are they stealing something?"

Miles collapsed against the wall and allowed himself to slide slowly to the floor. "They are," he answered, laughing aloud now. "Yes, yes, they are. You know what they're stealing? You know what, in fact, they already stole?"

His father stared down at him, his face bewildered, the pupils in his amber eyes as sharply cut and dark as bullet holes.

"They stole your son, Miles. You remember Miles? Little Miles? Cute little lovable Miles? Miles is gone!" He tunnelled his hands and called into them in an echoey way, "Bad men! Bad men! Heeelp! Heeelp! *Miles is gooone!*"

Miles was struggling to his feet, eclipsed by sadness, though a ghost of a grin still clung to his face, when he saw a momentary shadow above his shoulder. Something hard, something like a sockful of marbles, grazed his cheekbone.

"Fools!" his father howled, his blue-veined fists flailing the air. "Give me my son! *Fools!*"

Miles bent sideways, cradling his grazed cheekbone in both hands, staring up at the old man.

"Leave me alone!" he yelled, backing away. "Leave me alone! You old *fart*! Your brain is gone! Did you hear that? Did you *know* that? You're stupid! *Your brain is gone! You had a stroke and now you're stupid!*"

• • •

"What's going on?" his mother asked, switching on the too-bright overhead light. "Why'd you leave him alone? For heaven's sake! He's got himself worked into a lather! He's gone and wet himself. Why aren't you out there with him? He thinks you're gone. He thinks something happened to you!"

She glared down, gobble-faced, while Miles blinked against the light.

"You can't just forget about him! I left you in charge!"

"He punched me, or kicked me. I don't remember." Miles cradled his injured cheekbone in one hand and raised his other hand to shield his eyes from the light. "He's dangerous. He's nuts. My face is broken. He broke my face."

His mother rubbed her own face with both hands, knocking her glasses askew. "You know that riddle about the fox and the chickens?" she demanded, glaring down at him. "How the farmer's got a fox and chickens and how he has to row them across the river, but only one at a time? How can he take a chicken first, because then he'll have to leave the fox with the other chickens? How can he take the fox first, because pretty soon he'd have to leave a chicken with the fox on the other side? You know that riddle?" She glared accusingly at him. "That's how my life feels." Her hair was still undamaged, but her eyeshadow had smeared along one cheekbone, as if she had a black eye. "My whole life feels like that riddle."

"He broke my goddamn face," Miles countered. "He crushed a nerve or a bone. But you don't seem to care too much about that."

His mother straightened her glasses, disconnected her elaborate earrings from her earlobes. Abruptly she left the room, then returned with a bag of frozen peas.

"Here," she said, wiping her eye then examining his cheekbone. "It doesn't look too bad."

He recoiled when she touched him.

"Here, put the peas on it. Then come out, Miles. Tell him you're sorry."

"He *punched* me!"

His mother dabbed her nose on the cuff of her dress. "Tell him, Miles."

"Why? He'll just forget in five minutes!"

"Tell him anyway."

Still holding the peas to his cheekbone, Miles turned his head to face the wall.

"I brought home a treat, Miles. Doughnuts. Let's all sit down together and have tea and doughnuts." She ran her hand down his arm, but he pulled away from her. "Hold the peas there for a while then come out, Miles. You need to talk to him."

His mother stood beside his bed a few moments longer, then turned to the hoarse howl building in the living room.

"What *use* am I?" Miles heard his father say, weeping. "I'm no *use* like this!"

Miles tried not to listen, but still he heard.

"You're use," he heard his mother answer in her half-apologetic but stubborn voice, the same voice he knew she would have used to tell the bunker-builder he could not remove the books from the library.

"*What* use?" his father challenged. *"What use?"*

"You're company, Terence. I don't want to come home and eat these doughnuts by myself, do I? You're company for me and Miles."

"Miles," his father wept. *"Miles."*

Miles got up as quietly as he could and stealthily shut his bedroom door. His cheekbone no longer hurt, except with cold, but his chest felt scooped out, almost hollow. In front of the mirror he lifted his T-shirt, expecting to see a gouge, a wound, a gaping hole. But his chest was still regular, ribbed and flat, like he remembered. There was an indentation, though, a slight dip in the very centre, and he pressed his finger into it. Had this been here before or not?

He remembered his mother wanting to make a photo album for him. "Do you like this one of you and Dad feeding the chickadees?" she asked. "How about this one, where he's helping you build your model airplane?"

No. Nothing. *Nada. Nyet.* He wanted none of them. Why should he look at what she'd pre-selected in the viewfinder? Why should that matter to him? That was *her* picture, *her* life she was seeing. If he'd been the one looking through the camera's eye, he would have selected something entirely different.

He wasn't like her. He wasn't the kind of person who let others tell him what to see. He was more like the man he'd heard of in the library. The man who didn't believe in memberships. The man who didn't let others do his seeing for him.

The clink of cups came to him from the living room. *Maple,* he heard his mother say, *chocolate.* Then, *Aren't the rainbow sprinkles pretty?*

Miles switched off his light, then lay down again. He wished for Cleo, but she wasn't in his room.

From the window of the old apartment, he could watch traffic helicopter lights tracing jaggedly across the sky. Once, from his penthouse window, Jack had seen a real UFO and had gazed directly into the eyes of the silvery creature within.

Jack said it was awesome.

It was quiet now in the living room, completely still.

Miles looked out through his splattered street-level window. It was raining harder now, and no one, not even a dog walker, was out anymore. Two cars hissed past on the pavement, then a cab, trailing ribbons of coloured light. Next there was a bus, with its sweeping black wheels and its splendid commotion of air brakes, the people in its lit-up windows free in the world, and going somewhere.

wish

Zoe's mother, Kendra, is talking about Victor again. They are eating a supper of cornflakes and milk at the kitchen table, the light off to avoid the incubator effect of the overhead bulb.

"So you see, sweetheart," Kendra says, "Mommy's not going to marry Victor after all. Funny, isn't it?" Her hair is down, her face featureless in the half dark. "Don't you think it's funny, lamb chop? The way things work out?"

Zoe raises her arm from the shoulder as she hefts cereal to her mouth, her mind elsewhere, on dragons to be exact, dragons whom at this moment she sees battling in the growing darkness, over blue-black mountains.

The larger dragon has an immense wingspan, but the smaller one has a treacherously horned tail, which it can—and does—use as a mace. The larger dragon slashes downward with enormous talons, while the smaller dragon, less powerful but more agile, arcs its body upward and strikes again with its punishing tail.

Zoe feels the push and pull of her mother's voice, hears its tweet and twitter. The insistent rub of it creates a kind of static electricity that foretells a change of weather over the purple mountains.

"I mean, it's quite a change, isn't it? Not having ol' Vic around." Kendra laughs aloud, a half-hearted bleat from an exhausted whoopee cushion. She spends most days now lying on the couch in the living room, lights off, curtains drawn, the phone beside her, should Victor call.

Sometimes the phone rings, but most times it is the language school and Kendra goes in to fill in for one of the other ESL teachers. Vacation days were laid out back in February, and she is officially on vacation now. When she comes home, she goes back to the living room and lies down beside the phone again.

Zoe stares blankly at her, hears again an enormous leathery wing drumming the air, sees the fire of the large dragon's nostrils illuminate the pale orange belly and the garnet-red eyes of the smaller dragon.

"What do you think of it, cupcake? The way things have turned out?"

The small dragon feints left, right, plummets downward, whaps out full force with its dreaded tail. The large dragon bucks backwards, smearing fire across the sky. Then, just as the beast opens its mouth to bellow, Victor's putty-coloured face imprints itself across the purple distances.

Victor. With his stupid dinners and his ticking clocks. Victor. With his golden-haired children—Sam and Pam? Blixen and Dixen?—the rhyming twins who ping-pong jokes to one another, players on the home team, cuckoos in the nest.

"I don't care!" Zoe says, her eyes blinking rapidly, her skin prickly with irritation.

"You must feel some way, though, sugarball," Kendra prompts. "You might be a little relieved, I'm guessing. Are you relieved that Victor is out of the picture now?"

"I seriously don't care!" Zoe says, slamming down her spoon and feeling the answering spit of milk against her wrist. A soggy cornflake is stranded on her tonsils and she has to swallow several times to get it down. She puffs out her breath, shifts heavily in her creaky bamboo chair, clenches her toes around the chair rung, glares over her mother's shoulder.

"So what about our holiday?" she says at last. "What about the island where Diana is buried? We're still going to see the island where Diana is buried, aren't we?"

"No, cupcake, we are not," Kendra says. She is wearing a limp gauzy nightgown, the same one, more or less, she has worn all summer, but her voice is suddenly brisk, crinkly as Cellophane. "We're not going to England with Victor and his children. We're not going to meet his rich sister, or her handsome hubby, or their dogs, or the damned aunties either. The whole thing is off. All of it."

An immense silence wells up in the room, as around two dragons silently circling each other above night-obliterated mountains.

"But you promised!" Zoe finally squeaks. "You said we were going to see the island where Diana is buried! You said we'd go there! You said we would go on that boat and across the river to the island and see the dead princess! *You promised!*"

"Things have changed." Kendra rises like a ghostly figure from a lake, her back very straight, picks up her bowl, places it carefully in the sink.

Zoe gulps an enormous breath, takes in an even bigger one. She's only dimly aware of her chair clattering down as she heaves herself full-length to the floor, pounds her arms and legs.

"I want to go!" she shrieks, while bowls and spoons vibrate on the table overhead. *"I want to go!"*

Her mother remains motionless beside the sink. When she speaks, her voice crackles, like ice dropped into a drink. "Well, excuse me. *I* was the one who wanted to go, remember? *You* were the one who didn't. *You* were the one who fought against it tooth and claw."

"I did so want to go!" Zoe yells, raising her cheek from the sugar-sticky floor. "I did *SO*!"

"Yet you couldn't stir yourself to be halfway pleasant to Victor."

"I did *so* stir myself!"

"Is that what you call it? When you folded your arms at his birthday dinner and glowered at everyone from behind your hair!"

Zoe's breath comes in hot, hard puffs from her entrenchment on the floor.

"You wouldn't even learn the names of his children!" Kendra accuses. "*Dan. Ann.* Face it. How hard can that be? They're in your own class at school, for pity's sake!"

"Only for *gym*!" Zoe yells back, still face down on the sugar-gritty floor. She has been making potions all afternoon—red Kool-Aid for Courage, purple for Honour, as well as various other secret combinations for Stealth, Speed and the Ability to Change Form.

She hears her mother's bare feet unstick from the linoleum floor as she steps over her, unstick again as she gets ice cubes from the freezer. She hears her mother dropping ice cubes into the glass, the glug-glugging of a liquid overtop. She hears the ice cubes pop and tinkle.

Zoe feels the sandy granules on the floor pressing into her cheek. How has she come to be lying, lost and alone, her wings torn, her body almost lifeless, on this vast, dark and uninhabited desert?

The fridge door slams, then rebounds open again. The light bulb inside is a pale and heartless moon.

•　　•　　•

"Listen to this!" Kendra calls out from the doorsill where she is reading a magazine. She looks toward Zoe, who is lying across three kitchen chairs, a book with dragons on the cover inches from her face.

"My horoscope. Listen." Kendra lifts her eyebrows, then reads aloud. "*'You don't like change, but take a closer look. Your life can be so much better if you just give in to the opportunities. You have a wonderful memory, but don't continue to live in the past. Grab the present and embrace new opportunities.'*

"Embrace new opportunities!" She looks up at Zoe, her eyes wide. "Don't continue to live in the past! Zoe? I ask you! Is this me or is this *me*?" She cuts out the horoscope, tapes it to the refrigerator door. "Fasten your seat belt, sweety-cakes!" She winks at Zoe and pumps her fist in the air. "Your mommy's off to find herself a brand new boyfriend!"

Kendra tears down the living room drapes, paints the walls a colour called Pomegranate. She takes Zoe to a department store downtown, where Kendra models a leopard print miniskirt.

"What do you think?" says Kendra.

Zoe, one finger marking her place in her book, looks up. "It's pretty, Mommy."

"But is it pretty-pretty? Or va-voom! pretty?"

"Uh," says Zoe, her mouth open, her eyes dropping to her book again. "Va-voom, I guess."

In another alcove of the store there is a collection of candles, scents, creams and bathrobes.

"That is part of our aromatherapy line," says the clerk.

"Mmmm," says Zoe, leaning forward to smell the brown candle. "Cinnamon buns!"

"Cinnamon and vanilla," says the store clerk. She looks about her, steps closer, lowers her voice. "You see, the cinnamon and the vanilla in this precise formulation nestle into the folds of a man's brain and say *home*." The woman's pressed fingertips spring open. "Men are powerless to resist."

Kendra opens her purse and the clerk wraps the candle in a bed of tissue.

At home, they set the brown candle on the coffee table in the Pomegranate living room. That evening Kendra dyes her hair with a gel that leaves her hair the colour of new pennies, her palms the colour of tea.

•   •   •

Zoe opens the back door to find Kendra fluffing out her cloud of coppery hair and tending the barbecue on the back-yard patio. Heat radiates from the barbecue, from the colour-less cardboard lid of the sky and from the concrete tiles on the ground. Tomato vines droop like prisoners in their cages.

"Zoe, meet Kris," Kendra calls over her shoulder. "Kris, meet Zoe."

Zoe squints into the sunlight, her hand on the door latch, and watches while a grey-haired man appears, fading into existence by degrees, like a Cheshire cat—blue eyes, bushy eyebrows, voluminous Bermuda shorts, pilled woollen socks pulled up beneath bony knees.

"Manners, sugar plum!" Kendra's voice is bright as foil, her smile dazzling, her coppery mass of hair almost on fire in the sunlight. "Say hello to Kris, Zoe."

"I am so sorry! I didn't know," the man exclaims. "I didn't know you had a child." Then he sweeps one hand into the air, dips elaborately, kisses the air above Zoe's hand. "Little One," he murmurs gravely.

Zoe stares. She thinks of sorcerers, of travellers criss-crossed with secrets, of princes in disguise.

With much unwrapping of damp newspaper, Kris reveals a bouquet of flowers—dahlias, red and yellow.

"The phone! Is that the phone?" Kendra cries out when something rings inside the house. She turns off the gas, drops the tongs. "The phone! I'll get it!" She dashes in, snagging her lacy top for a frantic moment on the aluminum door.

Kris glances through the screen window and stiffens. "Something!" he stammers, holding the dahlias aloft. "Is alight!"

Zoe scrambles up to the window, her feet on a plastic milk crate, her elbows on the ledge. In the middle of the coffee table in the Pomegranate living room, the brown candle gutters and flames. "It's my mom's candle," she says. "It's aromatherapy."

The scent of cinnamon and vanilla wafts out, blending

with the smell of hot plastic tablecloth and extinguished propane.

"Kris is a doctor, Zoe," Kendra says, opening the lid of the barbecue when she comes out again. Her mouth smiles beneath the sunglasses she's put on inside the house, fine lines radiate from the corners of her blanked-out eyes. There is an eruption of smoke and heat and crackling from the barbecue, and from the house the scent of cinnamon. "Kris is a doctor from Poland. You will soon have your accreditation to be a doctor in Canada," she says, lingering pleasurably over the words *doctor, accreditation*. "Isn't that so, Kris?"

"I'm a polish doctor," Kris says, pronouncing the word like *shoe polish*. "Let me say." He stands erect. "I am a Pole. But not a telephone pole! Ha, ha, ha!" He is still holding the dahlias and the newspaper, though lower now. He stops laughing, bows slightly. "Maybe this is not correct. Can I say, 'I am a Pole, I am not a telephone pole'?"

•   •   •

"Head up, shoulders back," Kendra says.

Kendra and Zoe are carrying their ice cream out of a neon-lit Dairy Queen and into a crowded patio area that is set off from the parking lot by a row of concrete blocks. Kendra leads the way to the only free table, grease-spotted concrete, which like the rest of the patio area is bathed in yellow anti-bug light.

She sits down on the curved concrete bench with her single-dipped cone, Zoe beside her with her Peanut Buster Parfait. They are dressed in their new clothes, the ones they bought for their trip to England: Zoe in grey T-shirt and shorts, Kendra in a black linen sundress that shows off her slim white arms to advantage.

"Summer in the city!" she says with a dazzling, determined smile. She sweeps her pale arms out toward the neon lights that bejewel the street, also against the cloud of tiny hard flies that hover despite the yellow lights. She shuts her eyes and breathes deeply, as if inhaling a rare perfume.

Zoe hunches protectively around her Peanut Buster Parfait and begins to scoop ice cream rapidly into her mouth.

"Is anyone sitting here?"

Kendra and Zoe look up. The man has wire-rimmed glasses and curly dark hair. He has a small curly-haired boy with him.

"May we squeeze in here on the other side?"

"By all means, yes!" Kendra exclaims, fanning the bugs away. "Please do!" She takes a moment to straighten the straps of her sundress, to take another lick of her ice cream cone. "Mmm-mmm," she says. "Isn't the ice cream yummy? My name's Kendra." She holds out her slim white palm. "Is that a banana split you have there? Why, banana splits are one of my all-time favourites! Tell me, how *are* the banana splits here?" Her words are lively, as bouncy as if mounted on springs.

Zoe stares hard at her empty plastic goblet. There are only

three drops of dark liquid in the bottom. This is, the small dragon realizes, the legendary potion created by the Last Wizard of the Third Kingdom of G'Faar. She places both hands around the goblet, preparing to drink, but some unease tugs at her.

Didn't the Last Wizard warn the small dragon of forces that would try to deflect her from her True Path? The small dragon will not be deterred. Resolutely, she raises the goblet high, lifts it to her lips and, with the aid of her tongue, drains the goblet of the power it possesses.

"And this is my adorable daughter, Zoe," she hears her mother's voice saying somewhere else, on some vast echoey plain. "A fantastic reader! A real bookworm! You're a terrific reader, aren't you, sugar plum? Do you come here often? This has been so much fun! What do you think, Zoe? Wouldn't it be fun to come here more often?"

The small dragon watches the goblet tumble from her grasp. She watches as her arms lift before her, cross in mid-air, then seize her by her own neck. Her claws, possessed by something or someone else, tighten, tighten, tighten, against her will.

"Awwgghhh!" the small dragon moans. Under the yellow light, her head falls downward to her chest and her forked tongue lolls out.

"Thanks a whole bunch," Kendra says on the way home. "That's quite a sight. A nine-year-old girl drooling onto her T-shirt."

Couples walk hand in hand under neon signs, panhandlers sit cross-legged on the sidewalk, cars roll past trailing banners of music behind them.

"And your hair!" continues Kendra. "We have to get it cut and styled."

"I don't *want* my hair cut! I don't *want* it styled!"

"You can't see a thing!"

"I can see everything I want to see!"

"Excuse me," someone interrupts, "have you seen a small white dog?"

"A small white dog!" exclaims Kendra, brightening. "I absolutely adore small white dogs!"

Zoe, walking rapidly ahead, can still hear her mother talking.

"Man's best friend! I can see why they call them that. Don't you?"

"You have to learn how to chat to people. You have to learn to be *personable*," Kendra says when she gets back home. "The world isn't total gloom and doom, you know!"

"He was just looking for his dog, Mom!"

"I'll tell you one thing, Miss Stick-in-the-Mud. We're never going to get a man in our lives if we can't lighten up and be a little bit friendly."

"We don't need one. We have one!"

"One what?"

"We have a man, Mom!"

Kendra stares blankly at her.

"Mom! *Remember?* We have *Kris*!"

•　　•　　•

The small dragon is seated on a cloud, a cooling grey cloud, an airy cushioned cloud that provides a headrest behind her head, an armrest that enables her to hold her book more easily. There is even a button to alter the breeze, should she find the temperature unsatisfactory, not that she does find it unsatisfactory. She thinks she will never find anything unsatisfactory about this cooling grey cloud of a car Kris has borrowed from his cousin.

From somewhere else, the front part of the cloud perhaps, she hears voices.

"So, Kris. My friends tell me a doctor makes a pretty nice salary."

"Celery?" Kris stammers. "Nice celery?"

"Money," Kendra says, speaking a little louder and enunciating more clearly. "How much money does a doctor make?"

Words like *accreditation*, *salary*, *contract* are washing over the small dragon when the doors of the cool grey cloud open and oven-hot air slams against her body. Her feet are on the ground now and she finds herself at a concrete railing beside her mother and Kris. They are standing in the blazing heat looking out over a scorched hillside of parched trees.

A hot wind rises up from below, another hot wind, it seems, from above. The small dragon stumbles backwards, totters, barely upright now. Her wings! She tries to raise her wings, but they have become limp and lifeless.

"Little One." Kris is there. He is handing her a package with a straw extending from it.

The small dragon places her parched mouth on the thin white lifeline. She thinks of the tomato plants on the back patio, how when she poured iced tea over them their green, hairy limbs began to rise in a series of audible snaps, releasing the scent of geraniums.

"Snap! Snap! Snap!" the small dragon says, straightening herself in little jerks, her wings reviving, her arms waving above her head.

"We're not going to be a little *pill*, are we?" Kendra says crisply to the overheated air.

But Kris's arms are waving over his head as well. "The trees! So beautiful! So green!"

"Okay, we've seen them. Can we go now?" Kendra's eyes are blanked out by her sunglasses and her hair has gone limp in the heat. Grasshoppers click from the summer-brown grass.

•　　•　　•

The phone rings and it is Emma, a girl from Zoe's class, inviting her to her grandparents' cottage.

Emma, Emma's father and Emma's father's boyfriend collect Zoe, and they drive all afternoon along freeways, then increasingly smaller roads, until they arrive at a white cottage beside a lake.

Emma and Zoe unclip their seat belts, run straight into the lake and fall down with their clothes on. They eat hamburgers, corn on the cob and homemade sundaes topped with chocolate sauce and Smarties. They read their books by flashlight, hear the cry of a loon echo over the lake.

"Would you rather fight a hundred-year-old dragon or a thousand voles with lances?" they ask each other. "Would you rather go on a quest with a Minotaur or a dark-souled Mage?"

In the morning, Emma's grandmother enlists their help in making blueberry pancakes. Everything is different here. People laughing and talking. Orange juice intensely *orange* in its glass. The smell of woodsmoke.

"We have a toaster like that at home," Zoe says. The toaster with the engraved squiggle on the side is the only thing she can see that is the same as what they have at home.

Emma and Zoe read and swim, swim and read. At night, someone lights a bonfire and everyone goes out to toast marshmallows.

When a star falls, someone cries, "Wish!" and everyone wishes.

Zoe doesn't know how to wish fast enough. *Mommy—* is all she gets to wish before the star is gone.

Emma's father wears the Champion Marshmallow-Roaster hat, and Emma's father's boyfriend tells a scary story, playing all the parts. A branch cracks in the bush and everyone shrieks, then they sing campfire songs to scare it off.

"Wish!"

Zoe clamps her eyes tight.

"Mommy," the small dragon says in a clear, quiet voice inside her head. "I wish my mommy was happy."

•   •   •

"Lady Aster," says Kris, reading the names of the roses. "Audrey, Portia, Kathleen, Mary Rose." Kris has taken Kendra and Zoe for an evening stroll on a cobblestone path in the Municipal Gardens.

As Kris reads, a handsome man in a suit passes kitty-corner, and Kendra catches her heel in the stones and stumbles prettily into his path.

"I'm so sorry! Please excuse me!" she says, dusting off his sleeve.

Beyond the banks of roses, and across the broad lawns, flowery shapes of a wedding party drift past each other. There are torches and music, a bride who floats across the lawn like a large white moth. In a pool, bronze frogs spout water at one another. Just under the surface, carp glitter and glimmer like ominous stars, like mermaids gone wrong.

"Sarah, Ann-Marie," Kris continues reading, "Caroline of Monaco, Princess Diana."

"Princess Diana!" says Zoe, turning to Kris and her mother. "Which one? Where?" She looks down to see the bare stems and thorns of the rose bush, mottled pink and white petals lying on the cobblestones. The petals, when she picks them up, seem still faintly living and as soft as skin. "Is this like that place?" she asks, dropping the petals into her pocket and turning to Kris. "*Is it?* Is it like that island where Diana is buried?"

Kris stops walking, brings his fingertips to his lined face. "Water, flowers, stars," he says. "Little One, this is *very much* like the place where the princess is buried."

"But why isn't there a *Kendra*?" pouts Kendra. "I want a rose named after me."

"I will develop such a rose, my darling. I will find it and it will be named *The Kendra*! It will be the fairest rose—"

"Is that the second or the third wedding we've seen tonight?" Kendra asks.

"Mommy! Kris! Look what they gave me," Zoe says, her hands high in the air, her mouth full of cake. She holds up a piece of cake in one hand, a handful of sparklers in the other.

In a small cobbled courtyard between the fish pond and a bank of roses, Kris searches his pockets for matches, lights a sparkler for Zoe.

The carp have the cake, and Zoe is spinning, scribbling loops and zigzags of gold onto the air.

"You do it, Mommy! It's fun! You do it!"

"Not now, sugarcake."

But Kris has lit two sparklers and is already handing one to Kendra, the other quickly to Zoe.

"You have to spin!" Zoe tells her mother, demonstrating. "You have to turn around!"

Kendra holds the sparkler at arm's length, shuts her eyes for a moment as if making a wish. Then they are both spinning, writing their names in sparkles on the evening air. In the edge of her vision, Zoe sees her mother's dark shape spinning wildly, hair flying, arms waving but in rhythm with her own.

The dragons, the big and the small, are dancing, their wings outspread, their forms magnificent against the purple sky. Ribbons of light catch them up, entangle them, swirl them, lifting them high into the dusky air.

Zoe turns her laughing face toward the stars. "Look!" she shrieks, calling witness from the roses, from the thick-lipped carp, from the wedding guests, from the sprinkling of stars, from Kris who stands almost invisible on the edge.

Zoe stops spinning, breathless now, watches their names on the air, where they hover for just the smallest fraction of a moment before they disappear.

Kendra   Kendra   Kendra
    Zoe   Zoe   Zoe

Wishes. Wishes. Fiery scribblings on the darkening air.

cobalt **blue**

Iris is lying on the floor, listening to her messages, and extending her troublesome foot, to the left, to the right, to the left again. She watches it stretch and flex, swoop and glide, fly like a bony bird across the ceiling.

(The first message is a request to book her for supply teaching.)

How happy and hopeful her foot is, now that it has been freed from its prison of tightly laced black leather. She really must exercise it more regularly, she tells herself.

(The second message is from the people who keep calling to tell her she's won a free vacation—her own fault, for she's encouraged them once, by trying to claim it.)

Maybe with enough attention her foot can regain its former architecture. Why not? Okay, so she used to go running in five-dollar runners, but she's seen the error of her ways. *She repents!*

Surely she won't be banished to orthopaedic shoes forever. Visions of the wisps of shoes she will wear fly to her head. Strappy summer sandals. Maybe a pair of those blood-red suede boots she saw a woman wearing at the bus stop.

(The third message is from the bull-terrier-tenacious woman named Neesha, who is calling from the Riverdale Community Centre to remind Iris, yet again, that she is speaking to their lecture group this evening.)

Iris has not forgotten. She had, in fact, circled this date on her calendar when she was originally invited three months ago, and the carelessly scrawled *O* has glowed in a low-wattage way through the intervening days, like a dashboard Jesus or the exit light in a cheap hotel.

Now, however, rising from the floor to stir the soup and look out into the blustery darkness clotting the sky outside her window, then inside, at the buttery yellow reading light over her red velvet couch, Iris can only think one thing. Why?

Why has she agreed to give up her precious evening? Why did she not defend the solitude she craves after a day of supply teaching? Why should she have to travel across town to entertain this klatch of idle women who appear to believe she's been placed on earth for this sole purpose? *Why?*

The answer, as it happens, springs readily to mind.

Because she'd wanted to, that's why. Because she'd been pleased, even heartened, to be asked.

Iris is a painter. A painter who hasn't been able to complete a painting in almost four years now. Not unless you count the dreary little landscapes and still lifes she's been doing, not unless you count the ones she's stamped underfoot, the paint barely dry, the canvas tearing with the snarl of a Rottweiler, the snap of a spaniel (or sometimes, it seemed, the whimper of the tamest, lamest and most diminutive lapdog).

Nothing she does feels like her own work. Every piece feels like Mary Pratt on drugs, Greg Curnoe with migraine, Joyce Wieland locked inside a broom closet. Or a baby playing with its porridge.

Not a single piece contains her own DNA.

So, somehow it was inevitable, as sun, the rain (as chicken, the joke), that when she was asked by the woman at the Riverdale Community Centre to talk about her life as a painter, she readily agreed. ("A painter? A painter's life? Yes, I think I can talk about that!") She stepped forward into the folds of the rather becoming mantle they were holding out for her.

After all, she *is* a painter, is she not? A painter with a painter's not always easy life. A painter with a future wherein she will surely, well . . . *paint*. The *O* on the calendar seemed a quiet testament to that. The barely glanced-at *O* on the calendar made that quick passage past her closed workroom door a little less fraught.

Now, however, the time has arrived when she must pay for that bit of vanity. She has now to forgo her long bath, her quiet restorative evening.

The jig, in short, is up.

Iris eats her lentil soup, replaces hoop earrings with the more showy turquoise, brushes cat hair from her black pants. (She tried, for a time, to buy clothes to match the cat, but funnily enough, the cat hair, which showed up beige on black clothes, showed up black on beige clothes.)

It is time for the orthopaedic shoes again. The cat ambushes her from the closet and battles her for possession of the black laces. Iris matches her, tug for tug, and they are quickly launched into a ferocious tussle that ends abruptly when the cat bites Iris's knuckle.

"Beat it, brat!"

She runs cold water over the injury, applies a large, irregularly shaped Elastoplast. (So much for the glamorous image.)

She picks up a hastily dusted case containing a reel of slides in her left hand, a slide projector in her right—she used to do this sort of thing and still has the paraphernalia in the back of her hall closet. But her foot protests.

There has been no mention of payment. A taxicab is out of the question. She heaves the slides and slide projector back into the maw of the closet, locates a magazine that once featured her work, puts it into her bookbag. This will have to do.

She is about to open the door when she turns back. She opens her workroom door, entering as furtively as a banished lover, retrieves a stack of postcards created to promote a long-ago showing, slides them into her bag as well.

"Spare me your smugness," she says to the cat, who is

sitting teapot-style on the back of an armchair and revving its motor. She lifts the sturdy strap of her Mountain Equipment bag to her shoulder. "We all know that you're quite the *artiste* these days, and *you* don't have to scramble."

•   •   •

Iris knows what happened.

She was walking along the river one evening with Eric, the man she loved. The river was dark and fast below them, kayakers hurtling past like images at the edge of a dream. Purple shadows unfolded everywhere, and red-winged blackbirds shrieked as they darted out from the lush and darkening greenery.

She hadn't expected to fall in love again. She'd been married twice, had been in love more times than that, and had finally managed to talk herself into more or less believing that she was better off without a man in her life. (Why should she squeeze herself down to fit into the borders of some man's life? she asked herself. Why should she put up with being grilled about how much money she made? Why should she, for that matter, stock her refrigerator with bacon and iceberg lettuce and other foods she found practically abhorrent?)

Then she met Eric, and everything reconfigured itself. She slid her five-dollar self into a slot machine and came out silver and gold. The battened-down little freighter she'd been sailing through chilly northern waters reached another place, a river rather than an ocean, a place with warm winds, earthy smells, lively waves that threw back the colours of lights on shore.

How could she have forgotten? This is everything, she thought as they wandered down the dirt bike path together. The weight of his large, lovely carpenter's hand in her pocket, the way their fingertips touched, the way she sensed his presence like a dense dark continent beside her. Her entire life flowed toward this one moment. How strange to think that she'd once thought she could take it or leave it.

This is everything.

More than painting? a pouty little voice inside her head inquired.

But, turning her head, she nudged the question away.

What if— the stubborn little voice persisted. *What if you could only choose one? Painting or this. Which would you choose? Which? Which?*

Then, before she had time to choose, before she had time to consider whether or not to play along with this choosing, before she had time to ask why it was necessary to choose at all, her body chose for her. Her body simply turned, with the easy sweep of a weather vane, to face her lover. She looped her arms around his neck and, pulling him close, breathed in the wool smell of his jacket, kissed him on his mouth.

"I choose this," she said aloud. "Always this."

But a short time later, everything between them was over.

Eric returned to his former wife (a former wife who, it seemed now, had probably been more *wife*, straight and simple, than *former* all along).

"How can I say no," Eric asked, his huge liar's hands pointing one way then the other in the air, a policeman directing the heavy traffic of women bent on possessing him. "We spent twelve years together! You don't toss twelve years away just like that!"

Later, after the raging and the bargaining and the late night telephone calls were over, or mostly over, Iris found that the painting was gone too. It was sealed away from her like a moth behind the glass of a display case, like the knuckle of a saint in a jar. It had disappeared into the shadows like a jilted lover.

She had spurned painting, so painting now spurned her? Did things work that way? Wasn't that . . . well, too corny?

No matter the reason. It was gone. The difficulty seemed to be not so much with the picking up of a paintbrush (though even that had become fraught with difficulties, the way the paintbrush lay as heavy and clumsy as an oar in her hand, the way her paints lay inert and gelatinous in the pie tin, the way the white canvas yawned like an Arctic wasteland before her). Mostly, though, what was gone was her way of being in the world. There was a drifting, dreamy, slightly off-kilter way of knowing that was no longer hers. It used to be different.

She used to pull things in through her skin like a toad.

The world was all surface now, airless, flat, too brightly lit. She lived in a busy shadowless place, a place where her thoughts weren't her own, where it was always high noon.

She knew where she lived. She lived in a shopping mall!

Get a grip, she told herself. This was pure self-indulgence. This was nothing but a bad bout of hypochondria.

Okay. So, she chose, she reasoned to herself. Well then, she would just re-choose. This was all just a little bit of black magic she'd played with herself, some unlucky charm she'd stirred up out of the cobwebs in her own mind.

"Paint it," the psychiatrist whom she'd gone to see suggested. "Show me on canvas how it feels not to be able to paint."

Maybe what she needed was a witch doctor, she finally decided. (Though wasn't a psychiatrist supposed to be exactly that?) She paid one hundred and thirty dollars to a self-described shaman whose name she'd found on the bulletin board of a vegetarian restaurant. The young shaman came to her apartment with a CD player and played the sound of drumming while he bounced about in bright white Reeboks, moaning out a little song and swishing a smouldering wand of sweetgrass around the tables in her workroom.

It seemed to help, a little.

She tried to book a second session with the shaman, but he left a message on her machine saying he could only do one cleansing per death or, as in this case, end of relationship.

Death? End of relationship? What was he talking about?

Had he mixed her up with someone else? All she wanted was to reassemble the dislocated star map of herself.

And painting. She wanted that too. She wanted to paint. Never mind. She *did* paint. Sort of.

1. She painted her own greeting cards—birthday, get well, congratulation and Christmas.
2. She painted a white egg in a white egg cup beside a white pitcher, an idea she got from a novel she was reading.
3. She painted a skirt in shards of blues, whites and blacks.
4. She painted goldfish on her kitchen cupboards.
5. She worked through most of the exercises in the book called *Finding What You Never Lost.*
6. She drew one thing she liked: the shadow of a beet that was lying on her kitchen table. This was shortly after the shaman cleansed her workroom with sweetgrass and prayers.

She cut out the side of a cornflakes box, lined it with paper, dropped in a splotch of paint and a ball so the cat could paint. The cat did paint. Iris watched her. She noted the cat's deft, unstudied movements, remorseless and clean.

The cat was doing exactly what she *felt* like doing. How simple it was, after all.

Doing exactly what you felt like doing. So that—*that!*—was the key.

Iris hurried, almost breathless, to her own workroom, eager to put this lesson to use. But when she stood before her own paints and canvas, there was nothing particular she *felt* like doing. A line could go up. It could go down. It could be thick or thin. It could dribble and pool off the end of her brush. It was all the same to her.

Mostly, she found she felt like lying down.

The cat's paintings were interesting, some of them remarkably so, and Iris taped them up around her apartment. Sometimes she gave them names, like *Cobalt Blue No. 5*.

•   •   •

The bus is almost empty and Iris has an entire forward-facing seat to herself with a spare at her left for her bookbag. She arranges her feet, as she has trained herself, so there is no pressure on the heel of her bad foot.

In the art class where she was supply teaching today, a dozen boys stampeded from the classroom, shouting and laughing and flapping an open magazine over their heads like a banner.

"Our god will kill us if we look at this, miss!" they insisted when she went out after them to herd them back in.

Weren't they too big to be in school? she wondered. Several seemed close to six feet tall, and one was dressed in a black turtleneck and suede sports jacket like a young Hugh Hefner. Shouldn't they be out in the world, running falafel stands or strolling the decks of pirate ships?

Laughing and joking and bouncing off each other and

the metal lockers, they shoved the open art magazine in front of her.

"Look at this! It's gross, miss!"

"It's disgusting!"

The photograph in the magazine showed a painting of two pink, hairless creatures in a coiled embrace. Their bodies were earthworm shiny but static in some way, as lifeless as if made of wax. She sensed gaps in the horseplay around her. The bouncing and the banter were interspersed with mute bewildered half moments, when the boys hovered, transfixed by the image, waiting for her to say something.

"They're kissing," Iris pronounced, holding the photograph to the hall light.

"No way, miss! What's this?"

"That's their tongues. See? Their faces fit together like a kiss."

"That's not a tongue, miss! A tongue doesn't look like that! Look! See my tongue!" And the boy—one of the shorter ones—boldly stuck his tongue out, while the others hooted, staggering about in a show of laughter.

There was something disturbing, even to her, about the painting in the photograph. The tongues were small and perfectly conical, the same pink as the bodies. The faces were smiling in exactly the same way, their smooth shiny limbs stacked jauntily in front of them, like kindling or strips of candy. But the kiss itself seemed more a taunt than a true kiss. The kiss was mocking, double-edged, almost predatory.

She pulled herself from the photograph, but not before the vice-principal closed in on them, fine furry fronds of the poor murdered mink on her collar wafting about delicately in the breeze.

"This group is not in class?" she queried, her shapely eyebrows raised in feigned perplexity. "You are the teacher in charge, yet you've left the class inside unsupervised? Would you like me to review the correct procedure for leaving a classroom for which you are responsible?"

So it's come to this, Iris told herself as she returned to the classroom. She walked slowly in hopes of disguising the limp that had suddenly come upon her. My foot hurts when I walk, I am eking out a living doing work that is not my own, and I'm being spoken to high-handedly by a woman who is a good ten years younger.

Ten years younger and with nicer shoes.

•   •   •

They are approaching the part of town where diplomats' mansions rub shoulders with public housing, where silver-haired bureaucrats share the sidewalk with street people. Iris pulls the cord and climbs down from the bus onto the leaf-stencilled sidewalk.

A spit of rain catches her on the cheek, and her foot, unhappy again, protests. The wind flaps open her coat, threatens to snatch the tiny hand-drawn map from her grip.

Just ahead of her, a half-dozen bulky men in toques tumble out of a van into the rain and, glancing over their shoulders at her, vanish into one of the houses. If she's caught in the crossfire of a drug land shootout, she tells herself, that will be the absolute last straw.

She passes an upscale laundromat with an attached wine bar, an East Indian grocery store, the neon sign for a tanning salon. Then, when she has almost ceased to believe in its existence, she is there, at a large-domed church transformed now into its modern incarnation, a community centre.

The young man at the front desk, who is twirling a basketball on his fingertips, says he doesn't know anything about a lecture series.

"I'm sure I'm in the right place," Iris says, no longer sure and raising her voice to be heard above an old-time swing tune that is blaring from the next room.

The young man bounces the ball down to the floor, dribbles it a moment, then, scanning her eyes, pulls it up to his fingertips, rolls it across his shoulders, then lifts it, still spinning, into the air with his other hand. With a thrust of his chin he indicates the engagement book. Iris runs her fingers down the entries: *Swing Dance Classes. Power Yoga. Wreath Making. Wise Women. Board Meeting.*

"Do the Wise Women have lectures?" Iris asks, her eyes mesmerized again by the spinning ball.

"Could do," the boy admits cheerfully. All the lines in his body are perfectly upright, his spine, his forearm, his finger. Even his smile plays off the vertical.

Grinning openly now, the ball spinning again on his raised fingers, he looks over his shoulder to indicate a set of stairs, and she ascends. The walls of the stairwell are decorated with printed signs saying *Welcome* in different languages. *Welcome*, or maybe *Peace*. (Though who's to say some of the signs don't say *Beware of Dog* or *American money at par*? There is no one to ask.)

She tests doors, doors that are locked, a burnished wood door that opens to reveal a wood-lined study, another that opens to a broom closet. Finally she arrives at a door that is already open.

"Our artist!" someone cries out from inside. "Are you our artist?" A woman comes forward to introduce herself. She is Neesha, round, smiling, dark-eyed, younger than the other women in the room, less ferocious than Iris imagined.

Iris strips off her coat, accepts a Styrofoam cup of coffee from an aluminum urn. The eight or ten women, apparently rooted in different spots about the room, turn their faces toward her, pale-faced dandelions to the sun.

"Usually we have more people," Neesha explains, waving to the rows of metal chairs. "It must be the rain."

"Rain!" someone complains. "Tell me something new!"

There is a furious tapping on her elbow and Iris looks down to see a tiny bespectacled woman in a sari. "I was a teacher in India," the woman explains, pumping Iris's hand. "An instructor in advanced mathematics, and also physics. But now, in Canada, I wish to improve my mind."

"You can't watch-a the TV every day, every day," a woman with long bright yellow hair under a woolly winter hat explains in a querulous singsong voice. "You can't watch-a the TV *Mon*-day, *Tues*-day, *Wednes*-day, *Thurs*-day."

Iris waits to hear about the other days of the week, but nothing more is said. She sips her coffee, then smiles brightly. "Yes! Well!" she says, looking at her watch. "Do you usually sit down?"

They do as the teacher says and sit down on the clattery chairs, bunched up one behind the other—wary passengers in an unproven lifeboat—though the mathematics teacher sits gamely in the first row.

They talk about watercolour, versus acrylic, versus oils, about how much money artists make for a painting, about what money there is to be made in the sort of postcards Iris passes around. They take turns praising relatives who are exceptional painters and, while they are at it, praise the public library and the Internet.

"Why do you paint-a the same thing all the *time*, all the *time*?" the yellow-haired woman complains. She glowers in the direction of the magazine that Iris has propped open at the front. "Why don't you get new ideas from the Internet?"

While Iris searches for a response, there is the distant rumble of thunder and a scrambling sound from under the eaves.

"Pigeons!" someone pronounces.

"Filthy birds!" someone else calls out.

"They eat-a the bread, then they come dirty your windows!"

As if on cue, the wise women dive into a lively debate on the feeding of pigeons, though from what Iris can make out they are all on the same side, opposed.

A lipsticked woman with an apple-doll face and a shiny bright neckerchief tells a long, involved and seemingly rehearsed account of how she bought various plastic owls and snakes and whirligigs in order to discourage pigeons from roosting on her balcony, but how the pigeons laid eggs there regardless.

Someone else has advice about different gauges of netting suitable for screening off balconies, the advantages and disadvantages of each.

The question of disease is raised and exclaimed upon.

The East Indian mathematics professor explains that pigeons are not a problem in India.

"That's because of the *snakes*!" one of the women behind her indignantly replies.

At least two people have seen a television special on India and saw snakes in abundance.

"I bought a pigeon at a live-animal market in Chinatown," Iris interjects from her lectern at the front. "I drove it to a nice woody area out of town and let it go, but it just stood there. It couldn't fly."

The women turn to her in open-mouthed bewilderment. Perhaps they've forgotten she's there. Though, Iris reflects, the pigeon episode had been an admittedly bewildering experience all round. Not least of all for the pigeon, who moved reluctantly off into the undergrowth only when Iris clapped her hands.

Then, almost miraculously, the hour is over, or close enough, and Iris descends the stairs, her thank-you gift of a supermarket begonia, Styrofoam light, in her hands. Taped music—Chubby Checker—spills from the main hall, then mutes again as the door to the main hall closes.

She walks the length of the main floor hall and is halfway to the door when she sees him. She sees Eric standing by the door.

Of course, it is only someone who *looks* like Eric.

But then it *is* Eric.

He is standing by the doorway, his arms at his sides, one huge hand clutching his cap, the other one empty, and she knows he is waiting for *her*, declawed, docile, yet oddly ruffed up about the ears, like a rehabilitated alley cat, like a sinner who's seen the light.

An ocean sounds in her ears, and as she approaches she sees that he starts to smile his old smile, though he cannot be so confident of his charms as he seems. (Can he?)

His lips are moving, words are coming out. Through the sibilant rush in her ears, from his pink smiling lips, she hears syllables. She hears words she's heard before. The same words from the same mouth. "I." "You." "Here." "Tonight."

Her eyes move downward and she sees something she has completely forgotten. (How could she have forgotten?) She has forgotten his bitten fingernails, fingernails you never see him biting but that are bitten down all the same, his fingers blunt and knobbly at the ends.

As she walks, she gropes for composure, for a Joan Crawford mask of diamonds and ice. Fleetingly she is grateful for the turquoise earrings—for it is suddenly terribly important that he understands what a fool he is (what a fool he is! what a fool he is!) to have given her up.

As she sweeps past him, one hand holding the begonia, her other hand out for the door, she glances up with what she hopes is a glamorous, self-possessed smile.

But something is going terribly wrong with the smile, for she feels her lips—almost of their own accord—pull back, pull back, pull back yet again. She feels something like a hiss spiral up through her body, feels her hand, still holding the plant, rise to her shoulder then heave forward.

She sees intersecting arcs of red and black—the begonia tumbling off to the left, the pot to the right—and he is raising his elbow, lifting his hand to his cheek. Is it a wince she sees flicker across his face? Or maybe that same old smile?

She can't tell for sure, for now she is running—*bang-clunk*—through the heavy doors, down the broad wet concrete steps and into a rainstorm, bookbag thumping at her side, feet both bad and good (well done, my pretties!) carrying her down the rain-spiked sidewalk. The rain soaks her hair, runs its witchy fingers down into her collar, a cold wet leaf smacks her cheek like a hand or a mouth, thunder rumbles overhead, but she keeps running, the whole time sensing she is pulling the evening bag of the night—of a thousand nights—inside out.

Lightning cracks open the glass dome of the night, once, twice, three times. She pauses to gape, then runs on. She is a wasp, escaped through a crack in the glass, she is Lear on the heath—or maybe the Fool—she is a pigeon, flapping her wings against the storm. She is herself. That too.

She slows to a walk, trying not to thump down too hard on the heel of her bad foot as she walks past the purple and pink neon of the tanning salon, past a crushed pie tin snagging light on the sidewalk, past the laundromat, where a bicycle, overturned by the storm, shines a deep true blue.

Her heart stamps out its dance inside her chest.

I am myself. I am myself.

Her lungs gulp down the electrified air.

parcel for the **ukraine**

The bus stops at the Kentucky Fried Chicken outlet on the highway now, and when I get off, I can see all the way down the long block to my mother's house. Not only that, I can see my mother—who else but my mother?—pushing a very full shopping cart down the sidewalk in my direction.

I loop the handles of my bulky duffle bag over my shoulder and wave. I've come armed against the February cold of my mother's house with thermal sweaters, thermal long johns, thermal socks, even a polar fleece blanket. As I watch, my mother—still a half block away—stops and stares over the handle of her shopping cart. Then she turns her cart around and doubles back in the opposite direction.

The old bat, I think. I should get right back on the bus and teach her a lesson.

The bus is still there. The driver has just announced a twenty-minute rest stop, for this little town of Salt Prairie—

a baby boom town now, I'm told—is one of the larger centres in northern Alberta.

I keep walking along the long block behind her, though.
Trudging! Through the cold! I tell myself. Two figures inside
a woodcut called *Village Life in the Middle Ages*.

Which gives me plenty of time to wonder why exactly
I panicked at the frail, disconnected sound of my mother's
voice on the phone, delivered several sets of rock-shaped salt
and pepper shakers to a gift store on St-Denis, abandoned
my fourteen-year-old daughter to the care of the dog, then
rushed out here—at the cost, very likely, of a ticket to Greece
or Peru. All this to check on my mother.

My mother, who is obviously fine. My mother who, from
what I can make out, is in top form.

A few people from the Super-A supermarket we are passing take a friendly interest in this ragtag procession—my
mother, the scarecrow figure with her shopping cart, leading
the way, then myself, with my overloaded bag, half a block
behind. No one lifts their hat to offer me a ride, though, as
they might have years ago, before the surge of newcomers
the oil and logging industries have brought to the area.

The shopping cart goes as far as my mother's house, then
dips in through the fence and disappears behind the house. I
follow and the gate closes behind me with an uncompromis-
ing metallic *click*—a sound effect worthy of any prison movie.

"One more parcel to the Old Country," Mother is saying
as I haul my bag into the kitchen and through to the front

room, where I find a spot on the crowded floor for it. "I'm sending one more parcel. Then that's it."

Back in the kitchen, I embrace her awkwardly.

"So you've come to see an old woman," she says. Not one to show affection, she seems, however, happy enough to receive it. In fact, the oddly regal manner with which she accepts the hug—her hands in front of her, her gaze off to the side—suggests she takes it as her due.

"I thought I should come to see you," I tell her, sorting through various electrical cords on the counter before finding the one attached to the kettle.

I watch the way she edges along the kitchen counter to get the tea bags, then reaches to the table to transfer some of her weight to it before she sits down. She has become a child again, an ancient child, navigating along the edges of tables and chairs as she must have done eighty-some years ago, before she was able to trust her legs to carry her.

The grey, crumpled look of her, the way she creeps along, slow but stubborn, reminds me of something else too.

But what? Then I remember. She reminds me of an old cat I used to have. A cat who was old far longer than she was young, who ignored you except when she wanted something, and who bit you if you tried to pick her up.

Mother rummages about with the letters and photographs that are forever heaped on the kitchen table. I recognize my own excessively cheerful handwriting on one letter, then see a picture of my brother, Amel, posed handsomely in front of a new house he is building. Mostly, though, this avalanche of snapshots and letters is from our relatives in the Ukraine. The photos show rows of cousins and second cousins, grand-nephews, great-grandnieces, now mostly wearing Western-style clothing, each one worthy, each one in obvious or less obvious need of assistance, each one staring, shyly or curiously, into the camera.

Mother slides two coloured snapshots across the table. "From the village where I was born. My cousin's son's boy."

The boy in the first snapshot is dark, handsome, about the same age and colouring as my daughter, Daisy. In the next snapshot his face is ashen and he is lying face up on a decorated platform on the back of a wagon. At first I don't understand what's going on. He seems to be in a play, or some sort of procession. Then slowly I understand that the boy is dead.

The wagon is being pulled down a dirt road by a tractor. It is a startlingly sunny day and the fields around are dusted with green. Saplings on one side of the road are in leaf. Mourners follow behind in the dust, some of them carrying religious banners.

"This is the same boy? What happened to him?" I am still stunned that the boy is dead.

"He had pain in his head. Then he died."

"Why?" I repeat it, louder, for my mother seems not to hear. "What happened? Did it have to do with Chernobyl?"

"They say here that his head hurt. Then he couldn't walk.

Then he couldn't see. Then he died." She extracts a letter from the pile on the table, unfolds a sheet of graph paper that appears to have been cut from a school scribbler, then translates aloud. "'Dear Aunt, I hope this letter finds you in good health.'"

"This is from the dead boy?"

"No. It's from another one. Boris. They say he's smart. They say he is going to school." She continues to read from the letter. "'If it is not too much trouble, dear aunt, I wonder if you might be able to send me a coat. Maybe there is one that your son is not wearing anymore. And if it is possible, aunt, could you please send a coat without any holes in it? Warm wishes, your grandnephew, Boris.'"

"A coat without holes in it? That's all he wants? That's easy. Send him a coat." (A smart boy! A living boy! Send him an entire suit!)

"I can probably find him a jacket somewhere," Mother allows, refolding the letter and putting it carefully back in its envelope.

The clothes for the parcel are arranged in knee-high piles throughout the kitchen, behind the door in the front room and at the foot of the bed in my old bedroom. They are not to be confused with piles of other things that are for the garage sales Mother has taken to having.

Sometimes she tells me on the phone that she is tired and doesn't know why.

"What did you do today?"

"I carried the sawhorses and planks out of the basement for the garage sale. Then, after the sale, I took them back into the basement. I don't see why that would make me tired."

"Can't you leave the sawhorses and planks outside?"

"If you leave a good plank outside, someone's going to take it."

The garage sale piles contain children's toys, knick-knacks, unfamiliar coffee mugs, a plug-in jack-o'-lantern, plastic jewellery, a knitted candle. (A knitted candle! Shouldn't the knitted candle be enshrined in some collection of Completely Insane Things somewhere?) I recently learned that my mother likes to attend other garage sales, buy certain items cheaply, then resell them at her own sale. This is something that has blossomed late, this entrepreneurial side of her.

I open a small plastic barrel from a garage sale pile to see if it contains the small plastic monkeys usually sold in this container. My daughter, Daisy, has been hoping to get a barrel of such monkeys so that she can pin them to her knapsack. But this plastic barrel contains only a dozen very short pencil stubs. The price tag on the barrel reads eighty-nine cents.

• • •

"Power of attorney," my brother, Amel, said on the phone when I was preparing to come. "Retirement home. Three square meals a day. A complete roster of recreational activities." Amel is the owner of a successful car dealership in a town eight hours to the south. When we were young and had the opportunity to go to the lake, even before running into the water, Amel would take stock of the beach, then spread out his beach towel in the exact centre.

"But what about her garden? And her garage sales?"

But Amel doesn't like to be reminded of how our mother pushes a shopping cart around town to get groceries, pick up mail or pay utility bills, always on the lookout for a plastic pail or a discarded lawn ornament she can pick from the street or from some back alley to sell at one of her garage sales.

Amel and his wife bought Mother a proper walker once, a neat little pushcart with a small basket at the top that could be flipped down to create a seat to sit on. But Mother refuses to use it (though I noticed last time I visited that she has somehow managed to carry it down into the cellar, where it remains stockpiled along with the other things there). The basket is too small, Mother complains, the entire structure so light it feels like it could tip over. It is not nearly as good as a shopping cart. And who needs to sit down?

Besides, Mother doesn't like the way Amel and his wife gave it to her, unloading it from their motorhome and staying only three hours. "Like throwing a bone to a dog. Here. That's good enough for you."

•   •   •

"What's your doctor's name?" I am at the kitchen table, opening the phone book. "I want to take you to the doctor while I'm here."

"I'm not going to no doctor. What can the doctor do? The doctor gives me pills, but they're good for nothing."

"What kind of pills?"

She gets a bottle of pills from a drawer and hobbles over with them. She is wearing the same sort of clothes she's always worn. Shapeless brown pants. A pulled-out-of-shape sweater. Something under that, and likely something else under that. None of it all that clean, but not that unclean either.

Her hands are chapped and sandpapery-looking, nails cut straight across. Hands that are always chopping, hoeing, scrubbing, hauling. Hands, I knew as a child, I had best duck away from.

Hands, I realize now with surprise, that look almost identical to my own hands.

"Look." I hold my own hands up to my mother's. "Our hands are the same."

Mother looks warily at my hands, down at her own, then back at mine. (Again, the child and the wily old cat.)

"You work with dirt in the garden, and I work with clay for my pots." I'm not sure whether she hears me or not. But then, my pottery making has always been a sore point between us. Sometimes she refers to other girls in town, girls I went to school with, who, she says, have made something of themselves by becoming nurses or X-ray technicians.

(When I return from a pottery show with nearly the same number of pots that I set out with the day before, my mother's words settle down around my shoulders. What is required to become an X-ray technician, I wonder. How much training would it take to become one of those people who stick labels onto vials of blood and urine?)

I take the bottle of pills from my mother's hand. "It says you should take them four times a day," I say, reading the label. "Do you take them four times a day?"

No answer.

"Did you take these pills today?"

She pretends not to hear.

Louder. *"How many pills did you take today?"*

"I take maybe one a day." She seems pleased with her response. "If I get around to it."

"Take *four*." I point to the instructions on the bottle, a schoolteacher to an unruly student. "You're supposed to take *four*. Take four a day and see if that helps."

"The doctor doesn't do no good. The doctor only feels sorry for me."

"Why?" Louder. *"Why does he feel sorry for you?"*

"Because I took care of a husband. I took care of two children. And now who's going to take care of me?"

•　　•　　•

Seven days! I tell myself. What kind of lunacy was this, coming here with such little forethought and for so long? I am heading down the block to the Super-A in search of a box large and sturdy enough for the parcel to the Ukraine. (Thank goodness for a project like this to fill the time.)

Seven days, and all but one—two, once today is over— lie stretched out before me, a row of blank-faced tiles from the walls of an insane asylum. (Maybe Amel is on to something with his three-hour visits!)

The snow used to lie in four-foot drifts here. But that was before the logging industry decimated the northern forests, and the pulp and paper mills darkened the sky producing newsprint for Japan. The snow is sparse now, and what little remains lies curdled and crusted at the edge of the sidewalk, like a glazing job gone wrong. The famous blue sky is painted over with a splotchy wash of grey.

In Montreal, we sometimes see commercials filmed here in Salt Prairie, commercials for bread (or is it telephones?) that show brilliant blue skies, suntanned farmers and the last remaining grain elevator. Daisy calls me when one comes on and we stare at it together, truths and lies clattering together like discordant wind chimes.

I stop at the pay phone in the lobby of the supermarket and phone Daisy, in part to inquire whether the man came by to pick up the pot I crated before I left, and more importantly to find out whether he left a cheque.

"He liked it, Mommy."

"How could you tell?"

"He said, 'Oh.'"

"A happy *oh*? Or a garden-variety *oh*?" I fire my pots in dried leaves, pine needles, sawdust, as much of a scavenger, in my own way, as my mother.

"He peeked between the slats, then he sort of went . . . *'Oh.'* Then he walked really fast back to his car. The cheque is right here by the phone."

Daisy used to volunteer me for Go to Work with Your Parent Day every year at her school, and I would shepherd groups of children through my studio, giving them an opportunity to make finger pots that I would later fire and deliver to their classrooms. When Daisy didn't volunteer me this year, I asked her about it. She looked up from her math homework and said—a trifle abruptly, I thought—"They already saw you."

I decide not to ask her to sign the cheque for me and deposit it into my account, even though experience has taught me it's better to deposit cheques immediately. Daisy is the type of child who likes to do things exactly as they are supposed to be done. Signing someone else's cheque—even mine, and even if I've asked her—would make her tense and unhappy.

We talk about school, about a birthday party she's been invited to and about a dripping sound she hears, which, from what I can make out, is only the shower head in the bathroom. When I hang up, I make another phone call, this one to the airline, and shorten my trip by two days.

•   •   •

I pick up a bag of apples at Super-A, then linger over a showy display of Swiss chocolate beside the checkout counter. (With the new influx of money and people into Salt Prairie, anything can pop up on the supermarket shelves: kimchi next to the plastic lemons, grape leaves next to the cans of chicken noodle soup.) In the end, I pass on the Swiss chocolate then stop to examine the empty boxes lined up inside the front window. But the boxes here are flimsy and smell of pesticides.

The clerk at the drugstore next door says they have already crushed their boxes, and while the boxes from the liquor store are sturdy, they are too small for one of my mother's parcels to the Ukraine. The hardware store, I find, is required to return its boxes.

However, when I explain what I need at SAAN, the large discount clothing store farther down the street, the clerk says she may have something in the back.

"Doesn't the Ukrainian embassy give you crates?" the Filipino store clerk asks as she pulls a large folded cardboard box from the stockroom. "The Philippine embassy gives us crates to send parcels back home."

The warehouse-sized store is shadowy, almost empty of customers. Most people these days probably drive five hours south to the West Edmonton Mall to buy their clothing. In the West Edmonton Mall they can also ride roller coasters, eat in a submerged submarine, sleep in theme rooms decorated to make you feel you are in Rome, Hawaii or Las Vegas.

"We have to get our own boxes," I tell the clerk. "What do you send in your crates to the Philippines?"

"Last time I sent a toaster oven and laundry detergent."

"Laundry detergent to the Philippines?"

"It's cheaper here."

"We're sending clothes."

"They don't want clothes," a no-nonsense voice behind me says. I turn to see Wanda Walashen, the older sister of a boy I went to school with. "Your mother is sending another parcel of clothes to the Old Country?" Wanda asks. "They don't want clothes. They want money."

"It's going to cost you a lot to send a parcel all that way," I tell my mother when I get back home with the large folded box. "Why don't you just send the money? I saw Wanda Walashen at the store, and she said they would rather have the money."

Mother stares at me, her mouth ajar, her hands momentarily snagged by the air above the ball of yarn she is unravelling from an old sweater.

"We would of been glad if someone sent us clothes."

•   •   •

I make a supper of soup and sandwiches. Left to her own devices, Mother will eat porridge or discounted cake from the store. From what I can make out, she sells most of her garden produce at her garage sales.

The phone rings.

"Someone keeps asking for 'Mom,'" Mother says, holding the phone away from herself. "They keep saying, 'Is *Mom* there?' But *I'm* Mom!"

I can't believe this. Though, given the practice I've had navigating around my mother, I should believe it. I take the phone. "Daisy?"

"Dexter won't sleep with me." She sounds small and far away. Always, the dog has slept right beside her. "I call him, but he won't come upstairs. *Dexter*!" she calls. "*Dex*-ter!" She pauses. "See? He just ignores me."

"Take the bag of cookies upstairs. He'll come if he hears you rustle the bag."

I tell Mother about how Daisy helped me at the Christmas craft fair. "She carried pots from the car, helped set up the booth, then attended to customers. I could hear her saying things like, 'What price range were you thinking of?'" I smile, remembering Daisy's poised and ruthless salesmanship, so endearing—or so it seemed to me—in a fourteen-year-old.

"Then off she went to spend her own money." I am about to tell my mother how surprised I was by what Daisy bought: a cheap-looking piggy-bank made from a mould. But, just in time, I stop myself. It might be an occasion for Mother to point out that at least the piggy-banks (unlike my pots) had people actually buying them.

In half an hour Daisy calls again. "He ate the cookies then went downstairs again."

"Why is she calling all the time?" Mother asks. "What does she want? She doesn't need you. How old is she?"

"She's fourteen."

"Mother and Dad had to go sign some papers and left us alone when we were five."

"There were two of you."

"We managed all right. We didn't burn the house down."

•   •   •

"Someone took my shopping cart," Mother says the next morning. "It's gone."

"That's impossible. Where would it go?"

I pull on my parka and go out to look, but there is no sign of the shopping cart, no evidence of an intruder, no telltale tire prints in the crusty snow.

"Maybe someone from Super-A saw it and took it back," Mother says.

We look out the front room windows to the rear of the supermarket. A mishmash of apparently damaged shopping carts glint dully from behind an enclosure made of welded pipes.

"You wouldn't think they'd take it back without even knocking," I say.

Everyone knows she uses it to walk with. Who would take it away from her?

•   •   •

The huge cardboard box is open in the middle of the front room floor and I am rolling items of clothing tightly, jigsawing them in. A few of the clothes are new or almost new—work pants, blue jeans, sweaters—but some of the items are badly worn. Still others could pass for castoffs from a third-rate circus troupe in Croatia—tiny velvet skirts, see-through blouses, massive sweaters sparkly with sequins.

I step into the kitchen, where my mother is seated by the table. "Is someone going to wear this?" I hold up a sheer black nylon dress with a plastic gold belt sewn into it.

"If you don't think it's good, don't put it in."

"What about this?" I dangle a fleecy peach-coloured robe, the pile shabby and matted with wear.

"Someone could sleep under that."

"Where do you get all this stuff?"

She pretends not to hear.

Amel, who sleeps in his motorhome when he's here, said he'd gone out to pee and caught her going through garbage cans at two in the morning. But at the time I didn't believe him.

I return to packing, but something feels different. It takes me a moment to think what it is.

The air is calm and unruffled. Mother is not at my elbow finding something wrong with the way I am packing the parcel. (She had always been the kind of mother who grabbed the broom from my hands because I wasn't sweeping the right way.)

I look back into the kitchen and see her slumped in her chair beside the kitchen table. She's just sitting there. She isn't sewing a patch on something, or untangling string, or putting plastic spoons into some grungy bag for one of her garage sales.

I return to the kitchen and peer down at her. "Mom?"

"They say there was a boy and his father going on a boat on a river," she says, still in her odd listless state, beside the table. "They had the boy's grandfather in a sack."

"What do you mean, they had him in a sack?" I can't tell if this is a story from the Old Country or something she saw on TV.

"They had him in a gunny sack. I guess he was old and small. And when they got to the middle of the river, the father dropped the bag in."

"With the old man in it?"

"To drown him. And the boy said, 'Father! Father! Save the sack.' The father said, 'Why do I need to save the sack?' And the boy said, 'I'm going to need that sack to drown you when you get old!'" She grins up with her browned and stumpy teeth, rocking forward in her chair with laughter.

I look down at her for a few moments. "Is that what you think?" I ask at last. "Is that what you're saying? But we're not dumping you into the river. No one is dumping you in."

She doesn't answer.

I sit down on the other side of the table, over the letters and photos. "You're managing all right on your own, aren't you?" What am I going to say if she says she's *not* managing all right?

She doesn't answer.

"It looks to me like you're still doing all right."

Again she says nothing.

"You're still doing your garden. And your garage sales."

I can hear the defensive tone in my voice. Though what I'm saying is true, I tell myself. She shovels snow and carries enormous sacks of carrots and potatoes down to the root cellar. She clambers all over town with her shopping cart. (At least, she *did* clamber all over town with her shopping cart, until yesterday, when her shopping cart disappeared.)

"Don't you feel like you're managing all right so far?" I ask rather loudly. "Because if you're *not* doing all right, we should talk about that too."

Talk and say what? Where is Amel? Amel should be here helping me with this conversation. But Amel, of course, has washed his hands of both of us. "Don't say I didn't warn you," he said on the phone before I came.

"Who's doing so good?" Mother says. "I'm not doing any worse than anyone else, I guess."

"Do you have a coat for that boy who wrote? For Boris?" I ask at last. "Or should I go to the store and buy one for him?"

"Buy! Buy! Buy!" Mother says, batting her hand through the air. "For you, it's always got to be from the store! No wonder you never have any money!"

"Money? So now we're talking about money?"

I get up and go back to cramming pieces of cheaply made office wear into the box. So someone's going to wear a badly made lime-green suit with a coordinating hooker-style top on the wheat fields of the Ukraine?

I am so overheated, I stop and strip off a sweater. I know exactly how I could spend less money. I could spend less money by not coming to see her.

•   •   •

I'd planned to do this under the cover of night, but on impulse, in the grey light of late afternoon, I climb over the metal barrier at the back of Super-A and try to dislodge a shopping cart from the tangle of apparently discarded carts. I succeed in freeing one at last, but one of the wheels is jammed. I untangle another, and this one seems fine except for the child's seat, which has come loose and which could easily be repaired with wire.

But when I try to lift the cart, I can't raise it above my knees. I try to squeeze it between myself and the metal barrier and work it up that way, but it is still too difficult. I need someone to help. But who? Who can I ask to help me steal a cart from the back of Super-A?

I hear the back door of the supermarket open and, alarmed, I turn toward the sound. But it was only the door that leads to an enclosed refuse bin, and it bangs shut again.

It would be preferable to buy the cart, but I know that decisions like this are not made locally. No one here would be authorized to sell a shopping cart, even a discarded one. The head office would be in Calgary, or somewhere in Michigan. The plump and helpful manager I've seen inside would very reasonably suggest I consider a proper walker.

"Of course she doesn't like the walker," Amel's wife said, teaming up with Amel against me, as usual. "She refuses to learn the handbrakes."

Handbrakes? The elderly and infirm are required to use handbrakes?

Apparently so. The seniors I've seen with those neat little wheeled walkers must all be operating handbrakes.

There is nothing else to be done. I climb back over the barrier and walk to the front of the store, where I insert a quarter into a chained cart. Then I push it around the store, across the road and toward my mother's yard.

The cart is not easy to manage once I leave the pavement of the parking lot. It's large and unwieldy and wants to head off in directions of its own choosing. I struggle to hold it to my path, and it is only with some difficulty that I get it over the curb. Maybe this is a different kind than my mother is used to.

I push it around the house, hiding it as best I can in a grove of saskatoons that is not directly visible from the road.

"Your cart is back," I tell Mother when I get in.

"It's back?" She hobbles out to look. "Someone brought it back!" She lifts her head from her bent-down position to stare at it.

"Is it too big?"

"Did *you* bring it?"

"Yes." I am inordinately pleased with myself.

"This is the kind I like," Mother says. "It doesn't run away from me like the walker."

•   •   •

The next morning, Mother climbs up from the cellar with a light parka in her hands. The jacket is made of nylon, grey and trimmed with fluorescent orange, only slightly musty, only somewhat faded by laundering. It is a serviceable parka. There is nothing wrong with it. It is the sort of parka I've seen young men wearing.

But how nice it would have been to send the boy who asked—Boris, the smart boy! the living boy!—a brand new one.

I have the impulse to put a twenty-dollar bill in the pocket, and have, in fact, a new twenty, fresh from the bank machine, in my wallet. But what if the bus is late and I have to take a cab from the bus station to the Edmonton airport? What if my arrangements to be picked up in Montreal fall through?

I look at the faded grey parka, a skier on a small plastic crest sewn to the chest. Then I remember a tiny transistor radio I bought for Daisy at the local dollar store. I debate with myself a moment, then zip the radio into the pocket.

I am packing the parka in near the top of the box when I look up to see Mother hobbling into the room. She is hunched down low in her usual way, but is carrying something red and shiny—something almost ceremonial-looking—in her hands.

She has a box of chocolates, a heart-shaped box of chocolates, covered in red ruffled satin, its protective Cellophane intact.

It is only a drugstore box of chocolates—the sort that is discounted to almost nothing the day Valentine's is over—but in my mother's hands it looks intensely red, dazzlingly bright; it seems to have drawn all the colour, all the light, from this cold, cluttered room.

"You're sending *that*?" Inside my chest, my own heart is doing some peculiar reverberation with the red valentine-shaped box. "Where did you get it?" My eyes can't get enough of the redness, the brightness.

"Wanda Walashen brought it over at Christmas."

Mother presses the red heart-shaped box of chocolates into the top of the larger packing box, along with a list she has prepared explaining how the clothing is to be distributed. She places a towel over that, then shuts the lid.

I locate the end on the roll of tape, stretch the tape across the top of the parcel and down the side.

So, I find myself thinking as the tape screeches in my hands. So, she's had that box of chocolates tucked away this whole time. Interesting, then, that she hasn't seen fit to offer even one to me.

I pull the parcel onto its side and wrap the tape around the other way.

Not that I need those calories on my hips, I tell myself. Not that fake chocolate would be such a taste sensation. (How is it that I've got myself so tripped up over that cheap and gaudy box of chocolates?)

I've used up the tape and am now pulling a thin plastic cord around the parcel, vertically and across.

Never mind, I tell myself, still slightly dazed from taping and tying and mulling things over. Never mind. If I want chocolate—as I did earlier today!—I know what I have to do. I have to go out and buy my own.

Then the trucking company I called earlier is there, and the young man who drives the truck to Edmonton comes in. With immense cheerfulness and astonishing ease, he scoops up the parcel and carries it to the truck. Leaving behind the smell of snow, an empty hole in the centre of the room, and an intense longing in myself to be free, on the front seat of a truck and heading out on the highway like him.

"Make a list," I say, watching the truck pull away. "Of the things you want me to do. I have to go tomorrow morning."

"Go?" Mother looks up at me in a startled way. "So where do you need to go?"

"I have to go home. Back to Montreal." When I was out buying tape for the parcel, I shortened my stay by yet another day. "My plane leaves Edmonton at seven tomorrow night."

She is still staring up at me.

Surely, I tell myself, she can't have thought I'd come to stay.

Now would be the time. Now would be the moment to say, "Mother, think about coming to live with us in Montreal." I try to picture it, my mother living with Daisy and me and the dog in Montreal.

When I finally speak, it is to say, "I'll go get some groceries. And we should see if we can get your sink fixed." I had planned to do more. I had planned to install a handrail near the bathtub and another along the porch steps.

I bend down to pick up the scissors, and when I go to the kitchen drawer to replace them I am surprised to see my mother at my elbow. I return to the front room to pick up string and tape, and sense my mother, toddler-like, close behind. When I pick up the phone book to call the plumber, my mother comes too.

I find myself afraid that my mother will take my sleeve. I am afraid she is going to beg me to stay.

Don't say I didn't warn you.

I sit down at the table, the Yellow Pages open before me, and Mother, never one for closeness, sits close by me now, smoothing the tablecloth again and again with her hands.

Suddenly there is the sound of weeping.

But no. It is singing. My mother is singing a faltering fragment of some high-pitched, fast-paced Ukrainian song. Then she's explaining, all in a rush, about the teacher they had when she was in school here in Canada.

"He told us we couldn't sing Ukrainian songs," Mother says. "He said, 'This is Canada. You have to sing English songs. If you want to sing Ukrainian songs, you have to sing them on the other side of the river.'"

"Where was the river?"

"It was next to the school. My sister said, do what the teacher says. But I wanted to sing Ukrainian songs. So I crossed over to the other side of the river."

"Was it a big river?"

"Only in spring. So I crossed on the stones. I squeezed out the water from the bottom of my skirt and spread it around me on the rocks to dry. Then I sang Ukrainian songs."

"That's so brave." I can picture her with her wild blonde hair and the sulky, indomitable look she'd had even in her immigration picture. "How old were you?"

"About ten."

"That sounds exactly like you. Sing that song again."

I reach over for her hand. This is unlike anything I've done before and I find my breathing catch, for suddenly I am flying past the dark shapes of things my mother's done, of other things she's left undone. At one point my hand veers away, a bird toward the window, but then it's back again.

When at last my hand closes over hers, I am astonished. Her hand is surprisingly small. It is like a child's hand. It is as small and warm as Daisy's.

"Sing that song you were singing on the other side of the river."

I hold my hand over hers a moment longer. It seems a mouldery old bathrobe of a gesture, a heart-shaped box of chocolates of a gesture.

It is not enough.

It is what I have.

It will have to do.

I pull my hand away and Mother sings again a few lines of that song that sounds like high-pitched weeping. "It's about a bird that sings," she says. "Then, when it stops, there's only an echo."

I think of my poor dazed dust mop of a cat, which I never took to the vet until it was too late.

I think of the red heart-shaped box of chocolates, now in the dark, cold back of a transport truck on the first leg of its journey to the Ukraine.

We are still sitting in front of the Yellow Pages, but they are more grey than yellow now. It's only afternoon, but it is already getting dark, and neither one of us has switched on the light.